I0840688

SEARCHING *for* HIGHER GROUND

GEORGE GLEAN, SR.

KP PUBLISHING COMPANY

ISBN: 979-8-9857184-7-8 (Paperback)
ISBN: 979-8-9857184-8-5 (eBook)
Library of Congress Control Number: 2022906023

Editor: Delerice Mackey
Proofreader: Jazmine Jules
Cover Design: Juan Roberts
Interior Design: Jennifer Houle
Literary Director: Sandra Slayton James

Published by:

KP Publishing Company
Publisher of Fiction, Nonfiction & Children's Books
Valencia, CA 91355
www.kp-pub.com

Printed in the United States of America

DEDICATION

To My Children:
Cressada, Jamila and George Jr.

This book is also dedicated to:
Caribbean working people, at home and abroad,
who struggle relentlessly for dignity.

INTRODUCTION

When I was seven years old, growing up in Grenada, many people started migrating to England. The island of Grenada, located in the Eastern Caribbean, 515 miles northeast of Venezuela and 1529 miles Southeast of Miami. The island is known as the spice island of the Caribbean because of the variety of spices that grow in her dense forests. She is one of a group of islands called the windward islands, including St. Lucia, St. Vincent, and Dominica. Christopher Columbus, the Italian explorer, spotted the island on his third voyage in 1498 and called it Conception Island in honor of the Virgin Mary. In the 1520s, the Spanish renamed the island Grenada because it reminded them of Spain's capital city, Granada. However, when the French captured the island, they changed the name to LeGrenade, and when it was taken over by the British, it was renamed to its present name, Grenada.

At such a young age, I had no idea why it was necessary to leave and travel to the unknown. During those days, the trip to England was made by boat. The travelers would write back, after arrival, that all they would see for days was sea and sky. I thought that this would dissuade future travelers, but it didn't. As I grew older, these trips to England grew in frequency, and many more people were England bound. It seemed that not even sea-sickness or homesickness was enough to change their minds. More and more people swarmed the seaport, as time went on, to make the trip to England.

It became more than evident that no one wanted to remain on the island because of these simple yet salient facts: work was scarce, wages were low, everyone wanted to go. Most of the population, especially men, had to find a way to make a decent living for themselves and their families. Thus, *Searching for Higher Ground.*

The M V Windrush was an old merchant ship, that served as the first carrier of West Indians to England in 1948 with 492 passengers on board from Jamaica, Trinidad and Tobago and other islands. These West Indians were going to England to help fill the post second world war labor shortages. But much more than that, they were going to a country that promised employment and prosperity.   (photo: historypod.net)

CHAPTER 1

"This must be paradise," the old man muttered. He stood on the edge of a hilltop surveying the wide array of lush, colorful vegetation—different hues of red, many shades of greens, yellows, and browns—a multiplicity of breathtaking colors.

This remarkable and magical sight, which he'd once known intimately and taken for granted, reignited and illuminated all his senses. He smiled contentedly, seduced by the myriad of scents.

He looked youthful and exuberant. Although his white hair rose like a plume. A slender man, he stood about six feet tall. The flabby muscles in his arms had been muscular once. His face was wreathed with creases like a rumpled bedsheet; his forehead ridged like a laundry washboard. The skin on his hands was tight, hardened, and calloused. More lines crisscrossed the palm of his hands like a railway track system. If he ever had his fortune read, it would be a palm reader's nightmare. He was an endearing and intimidating man.

It was amazing he could still stand without bending at the waist. His physical condition was a telltale sign of a battered and beleaguered life. Nonetheless, his demeanor showed these hardships were no barrier to his indefatigable spirit. He laughed heartily—his voice no longer muzzled but firm, strong, and vibrant. With both hands towering over his head, he shouted for all creation to hear, "THIS IS PARADISE!"

Smiling, he continued, "I have traveled to many parts of this world, and I have yet to see any place come close to this little island of Grenada in natural beauty. None. When I say none, I mean none."

Watching my father's passion for his homeland, I felt a mixture of joy and sorrow. I was so happy to be reunited with my father after all these years but deeply saddened at the time we'd lost. I had to agree with him, though, that no other place in all the world could compare to the beauty of our little island. As children, one fact immediately introduced to us was our island was formed by volcanic activity. We were taught about volcanoes and their destructive nature and always were fearfully aware that our volcano could begin to spew deadly molten lava all over our little island at any time.

Our parents and teachers tried to calm our fears by explaining the difference between a dormant and active volcano, but that only confused us more. They said that some volcanoes are active while others are presumed dormant—still, there was an unpredictable potential they might reactivate.

Our questions were simple: Could this volcano erupt at any time? Or could this volcano never erupt? The answer was always ambiguous: "Yes! But . . . "

We weren't convinced. Nevertheless, we went about our daily lives unperturbed. Our parents, neighbors and friends went about their regular day-to-day activities with no noticeable worry.

However, there was one plus to the overall equation. We were happy to learn that the volcanic ash deposited long ago was mainly responsible for our rich and arable soil. In turn, it took credit for the island's lush greenery and its abundant vegetation.

This comforting news was always overshadowed when volcanic eruptions did occur on other islands. For instance, there was La Soufriere on the neighboring island of St. Vincent in 1979 and 2020; and Soufrière

Hills on the island of Montserrat in 1995. In the end, we learned to take life one day at a time and enjoy the good with the bad. We also learned; with the lucrative advent of the tourist industry, we were the envy of most of the world because of our climatic conditions, cool nights, comfortable breeze, and warm days. The average year-round temperature of 70- and 80-degrees Fahrenheit made it a joy to anticipate the mornings which came to life with the crowing of the cocks, squawking of tropical birds, and barking of wayward dogs.

During the rainy season, you might wake to the loud and vicious pounding of the waves of the seawater cascading off the rocks. In contrast, you can be lulled to sleep by the hypnotic, rhythmic sounds of the gentle lapping of the waves on the sandy shores of this never-ending coastline.

Growing up in this idyllic setting was a lesson in complete freedom. A carefree, laissez-faire attitude reigned: young boys—in shorts—ran about—shirtless and shoeless, while barefoot girls carried out their chores wearing torn skirts and tattered tops.

School attendance was compulsory for all children every day of the week, though some children always had to miss school on Fridays—often reserved for them to help their parents tote crops from the countryside down to the markets to sell on Saturdays.

These crops did not come from huge estates but from small parcels of land that were individually owned or rented. None of these farmers owned vehicles, and even if they did, the roads were like tracks, impassable to vehicular traffic. Forced to find an effective way to get their produce to the market, the farmers became very creative. They made cushions out of straw or cloth, called a *cotta*. Then, positioned them in the middle of the head and rested the load on the cotta. This technique alleviated the strain on the head and pressure on the neck. Produce was also piled in oversized baskets or *Croix-Croix* bags—huge baskets handwoven from the local bamboo plant.

The strands were woven, mainly by women, until a container formed to hold produce like mangoes, oranges, sapodillas, and grapefruits. The bags farmers used came from the local shops that traded in household goods like rice and sugar from as far away as Africa and Europe.

Like a well-orchestrated procession, men carried the huge bags on their shoulders and the women's faces were hidden under those huge, wide baskets on their heads. The boys had smaller bags hung over their shoulders, while the girls balanced smaller baskets on their heads.

It was a sight to behold.

The bags and baskets were unbelievably stable on their heads. It was a balancing act unmatched by any modern-day circus. They talked, laughed, and teased one another with such ease that it sometimes gave the impression they were unaware of carrying anything on their heads.

West Indian Woman carrying and
balancing basket filled with produce.

It was common to see a man holding a long stalk of sugarcane in one hand, peeling the skin off with a sharp machete held in his other hand—all while walking and balancing a basket filled with produce on his head. A woman with a wide basket on her head and wearing a long, flared skirt might swing in calypso rhythm as she meandered through a tiny track down a slight incline. Then, she'd stoop at a standpipe and drink water from her cupped hands. All these activities took place with the load seemingly glued to her head. Unbelievable!

Help was necessary when the load was placed on the head or removed at the destination point. The first action was called a *help-up* and the second was called a *help-down*.

After a hectic day of bargaining, compromising, and selling at the market, sellers looked forward to the rituals and rewards of Saturday night. These rituals were different for men, women, and young people. Every Saturday evening, the boys swept the dirt yards with *cokea* brooms, indigenous brooms made of the branches from the coconut or palm trees. The girls and the women worked in the kitchen seasoning meats, baking bread, peeling ground provisions, and cleaning rice—all in preparation for the biggest and grandest meal of the week, the Sunday Dinner. What about the men? Funny, you should ask. They were in the local rum shops, drinking with their friends and playing dominoes, cards, or checkers. At 10:00 p.m. the rum shops closed. Most patrons staggered home, while some had to be awakened from a drunken stupor, sometimes lying in a drain or a gutter. This could be likened to a ritual because these activities and behavior patterns occurred every Saturday night like clockwork.

General stores in the village sold groceries, sodas, nails, and screws but no alcohol. Another store merchandized sneakers, combs, brushes, and cloth by the yard used for making men's pants, ladies' dresses, and cushion cloth for living room chairs and curtains.

That was where the tailor and the seamstress proudly displayed their skills and expertise. There was one tailor in the village who employed about three apprentices. He designed and cut the cloth based on measurements taken from the customer. Then, he sewed the pants together. The apprentices hemmed the bottom of the pants or put a cuff at the end of both legs in order to adjust the length of the pants to the prescribed measurements. Their job also included sewing on buttons and making buttonholes. During the August vacation, the tailor received inundated job requests. Parents usually saved money during earlier months so their sons could get a new pair of pants for the coming school year intended to last until the next school year. At that point, the pants would be recycled or handed down to the younger sibling. Those same pants moved from school pants to home pants if there were no younger siblings. *Home pants* implied the pants were worn after their school pants were safely secured, allowing the children leeway to participate in more rambunctious activities.

The seamstress sewed dresses for the women and girls. Like her counterpart, the tailor, she took the lady's body measurements—the bust, the waist, the hips, and the desired length. The dresses were then cut and sewn together. Her apprentices, usually young girls, hemmed and sewed on buttons.

The seamstress gained status in the village based on the number of brides she outfitted with dresses. The irony was that you could easily count on your fingers the number of weddings taking place in the village each year. Marriage always incurred great expense—to most villagers, it was a luxury they could not afford. Instead, they were forced to live together in what came to be known as a *common-law relationship.*

On the other hand, going to church and following the sacraments was sacrosanct. The seamstress made most of her money by sewing outfits for the girls' first communion and holy confirmation observances.

Every Sunday morning, our mother woke us by yelling at the top of her voice, "You hear the bell? That's first bell ringing!" We had to be ready to go to church by the time the second bell rang in twenty minutes. No one liked getting up so early, but we all enjoyed getting ready for church because we got to wear our *Sunday clothes*. We may have worn the same suit every Sunday, but no matter what happened, we never wore that outfit any other day. This was the only day we were allowed to wear socks and shoes. Our entire bodies would be rubbed down with coconut oil. We looked and felt brand new. We would rush home from church, change our clothes, fold them neatly, and carefully put them away for the next Sunday.

Going to church was a mother and children affair. The number of men who attended church services on a regular basis could be counted on one hand. Okay, probably two—if it was Easter Sunday or if Christmas was observed on a Sunday.

CHAPTER 2

There were six of us in my family: my dad, Alfonzo, and my mom, Alberta. There was me—Sinclair, my brother Alfred, who was four years older than me, and two younger sisters. Elva was three years younger than me, and Marjorie, the youngest, was three years younger than Elva.

The community looked up to us because my dad owned one of the little shops, and my mom was the local seamstress. My older brother was four years my senior, and there was a three-year gap between the rest of us.

When I turned ten, I was groomed to take over my brother's acolyte duties in the church and some of his chores around the house. In addition to these new undertakings, I began to take extra lessons for the scholarship examination. If I passed this exam, I would be accepted to either of the two secondary schools on the island for the next five years, tuition-free. My older brother was attending one of these secondary schools, but he had not won a scholarship. Instead, he sat and passed the school entrance exam, which meant my father had to pay his tuition.

You would not believe the pressure my father exerted on me. "Sinclair, you are brighter than your brother," my dad would say. "And, besides, if you pass the scholarship exam, it would save me a few dollars."

Should I take the blame for depleting his pockets? I studied hard. I played less. I felt obligated to help my father keep some money in his pocket.

This was a problem soon resolved through a most unexpected turn of events.

During this period, one of our dad's dearest friends started visiting our family at regular intervals. I never knew just how long they had been friends, but from all indications, it had been a very long time. We called him Mr. Eric, and we called his wife Ms. Ann. They lived in the city, where we assumed they both ran a thriving retail business. I say assumed because they drove a relatively new car and were always nicely dressed.

The couple always visited on a Sunday. For one, the business was closed on Sundays. And two, we lived in the country about twelve miles away from the city. They referred to the drive as their "little weekend getaway to the country."

Mr. Eric was about six feet tall with a body to match his height. He was not skinny, but neither was he fat. Well built, proportionate, and had only a small protruding gut, he was beginning to go bald and wore glasses. But he always removed the glasses to make a point and put them back on just as quickly to congratulate himself on a point well made. He loved to talk, but in his effort to over pronounce and over articulate, he often sounded as if he had hot potatoes in his mouth.

Ms. Ann, on the other hand, was anxious to tolerate him. A short "yes, dear," always indicated she agreed with his points, and she kept a constant smile at the ready. Though Ms. Ann was just a little shorter than her husband, we described her as slim but solid. She always wore her hair plaited in thick cornrows, which exaggerated her forehead and high cheekbones. We all admired her. The consensus among us kids was unanimous—we thought she was a very good-looking woman.

However, we children were always uncomfortable when our parents' friends visited. We were especially annoyed at Mr. Eric when he sat down to eat with the family. Our parents taught us the rules of etiquette, and we were supposed to show them off when visitors or relatives joined us for a meal. We thought we knew how to eat with knives and forks with our eyes closed, but we always fell short when Mr. Eric sat at our table.

"Elbows off the table," he would shout with military precision. "No slurping your soup. It's not elegant." He would then take time out to demonstrate just how it should be done.

It also became a standing joke to see him pack the pieces of food onto his fork as if he were meticulously building a mini mountain. He would take the fork in his left hand and the knife in his right hand, hold the meat with his fork, and cut a small piece from the meat. Then, put some rice on top, and add a little *callaloo* over the rice. He would wipe the knife off the fork and put the food in his mouth. Then and only then, would his mouth open in order to consume the contents.

The whole action was like a caterpillar bulldozer emptying its load into the bed of a truck. Every now and again, one of us kids would let a chuckle escape, but we had to wipe the smile off our faces as soon as it came or we would receive serious consequences from our parents.

When drinking a glass of juice, Mr. Eric would lift it delicately to his lips to avoid making the hissing or slurping sound. I said before that we all observed the rules of etiquette, but Mr. Eric took it to new heights. He made it so exaggerated and deliberate; it was too mechanical. We began to tell each other, "There is no way anyone should go to so much trouble to eat." Mr. Eric became the butt of all the jokes, and whenever we were eating without our parents at the table, we tried to emulate him—but without success.

Overall, though, we thought he meant well and that both Mr. Eric and Ms. Ann got along nicely with our parents. I began to assume he was unaware of how we had fun at his expense. Truth be told, we would have preferred to spend lunchtime without him.

During this time, Mr. Eric began to take a disgustingly keen interest in me and my studies. *Why me?* I questioned. *Shouldn't he show more interest in my brother? After all, he was older and more mature. But no!* Our guest was relentless in his concern for my general well-being, especially in regard to my schoolwork.

My older brother, as I said before, was attending secondary school. He had to travel by bus to and from school every day. It was brutal on both fronts for my parents—they had to pay his tuition and his transportation bill every month. If I passed the scholarship exam, they would only have to pay my transportation bill. It would be, of course, a huge savings.

My father's friends were now slowly becoming family friends, especially since Ms. Ann and my mom were developing a friendship of their own. It was inevitable that they finally roped the children into the fray. They were no longer Mr. Eric and Ms. Ann—they officially became Uncle Eric and Auntie Ann, just so.

Uncle Eric immediately began to take advantage of his new title, making his interest in me legitimate. "Sinclair," he asked, "How are you doing in school?" His voice gleefully boomed as he pulled me to him with his big right arm. "We're depending on you." He poked my stomach with his index finger and repeated, more firmly this time, "We're depending on you, big boy!"

In the meantime, I tried to live as normal a life as any child. I used every chance to do as many fun things in my boyhood as my parents allowed me to enjoy. They let me go to the sea with my friends so long as my brother was there. After all, the sea was literally a stone's throw from our house. We loved to ride the waves with pieces of cork wood. Every so often we would get caught up and swirled around—we called this being *boiled* by the waves. Looking back, I could see how dangerous those sea games were, but we all survived.

There was another activity we did, which we all knew was extremely dangerous because fire was involved. This was called, *busting the bamboo*. But as kids, we always reasoned the more dangerous the activity, the more we wanted to be part of it.

The bamboo had to be carefully selected from a bamboo patch. The stalk was usually about five feet long and, like sugar cane, was divided into what are called *joints*. Each joint was approximately one foot long. The five-foot-long bamboo would therefore have five joints. We then used a knife or a sharp object to create a hole in all of the joints except the last one. Kerosene fluid was poured into the last joint through a hole at the top. We would light the kerosene and then blow air into the stalk. When the kerosene grew hot, the combination of the kerosene and the fire caused smoke to develop. We smothered the fire in the bamboo by blocking the hole at the top. Then, the accumulated smoke was blown through all the holes. The combination of kerosene, smoke, and fire being blown through the tiny holes in the joint of the bamboo caused a loud sound. When the booming sound occurred, the bamboo was busted.

Bamboo bursting in Grenada

(photo: shutterstock.com)

Needless to say, things went wrong on numerous occasions. Sometimes the hot smoke burned the eyebrows. In most instances, someone's mouth got burned. After all, the trick involved constantly blowing a current of air to get the fire to go through the holes, and our lips were wet with the kerosene. One wrong turn and the fire could light up your lips. The most rewarding aspect was although accidents could happen, they rarely did. But that booming, cannon-like sound? That was the ultimate rush.

That reminded me of one night during the Christmas season when we had a custom of getting together with a group of our friends and older acquaintances to go caroling. We went from house to house, singing Christmas carols in the early hours of the morning. After we sang our selections, the occupants of the house came to the door and gave us a monetary contribution or something to eat and drink.

We didn't experience winter temperatures, but being outside at four o'clock in the morning, we were forced to wear sweaters to keep off the cold morning air. The morning air was unusually cold every year during December.

This particular Christmas season, we were surprised to see lights on in many of the houses where we serenaded. Normally, the windows would be dark. If the occupant loved the singing, only then would the lights be turned on as a welcoming gesture.

We soon learned the reason all the households were wide awake—all ears were glued to the radios. The West Indies cricket team was playing an away test series against the Australian team. When we approached the fifth house on the route, everyone was screaming. We inquired as to the reason for the commotion and exuberance. Quickly, we learned that the game had everyone's riveted attention. We soon had to abandon our singing and became engaged in the festivities.

It turned out to be a truly momentous occasion. Mr. Hadeed, one of the few Australian supporters on the entire island, turned up the volume to his radio so we could hear the exciting ball-by-ball commentary.

The Australians were batting, and the West Indians were fielding. The Australian team had to score 233 in total runs to win. The score was at 226 runs for seven wickets at the time of all the cheering and screaming. Australia was in a winning position before the drama unfolded. It boiled down to one last over. West Indies with six more balls to be bowled, Australia with six more runs to win. High drama, December 9, 1960, and the venue was the Gabba in Brisbane, Australia.

Wesley Hall, the great West Indian fast bowler, was up to bowl. Jerry Alexander was up close behind the stump, daring the batsman to be out of his crease. Captain Frank Worrell had set a very defensive field in what was called *The Umbrella Formation*: eight men very close to the bat, one on the boundary line, and Gary Sobers, the ambidextrous master, at mid-off.

The Australian wickets fell, and the scores became level with two balls to go and the last wicket to fall. The score tied. Wow! What a "ting!" One could hear grown men's bellies grumbling from nerves and churning with fright. The commentator's voice rang out, "And in comes Wes Hall."

Wes Hall pounded in like a galloping horse on the last run to escape possible death. The Australian batsman defended the wicket with his life.

One ball to be bowled. One wicket to fall. One run to decide victory for the Australians. Or a tie for the West Indians. Wes Hall had one last delivery to Australia's batsman, Lindsay Kline. He played the ball to the leg side, and the batsman attempted what would have been the winning run. Joe Solomon, West Indian fielder, threw down the wicket, and Ian Mechift was run out.

Noise in the place! The match tied. Incredible! My group was shocked into an uneasy silence. Then, pandemonium broke loose. Almost simultaneously, every West Indian islander was joyous beyond measure. Australia was shocked. The world was befuddled. What were the odds?

For the first time in the history of the game, there was a tied outcome. Apart from gaining a niche in cricket history as the first test to end in a tie, this match will always be remembered with enthusiasm because of its excellent cricket. It was played in a most sporting spirit, with the climax coming in a tremendously exciting finish as three wickets fell in the final over.

Isn't it paradoxical that in 1958, only two years earlier, the West Indian islands had decided to form a federation? According to the Mighty Sparrow's calypso by the same name, they failed miserably. However, on December 9, 1960, the islands became more united than ever before. The West Indies cricket team made history. They made every person on every West Indian Island very proud.

The first-ever tied Cricket Match.

For a short period of time, the West Indies cricket team of eleven men with varying backgrounds and from different islands achieved the federation that the scholarly politicians were unable to attain.

That night, our instruments stopped playing ancient Christmas carols. Instead, the guitars strummed a pulsating calypso tempo, accompanied by bottle and spoon percussion, gyrating hips, and flayed arms. We sang along with calypsonian David Rudder as we all, in earnest, rallied around the West Indies.

CHAPTER 3

Uncle Eric and Aunt Ann paid a rather impromptu visit one day. They had already visited on Sunday, and here they were returning on Thursday. My parents were home because most business establishments only opened for a half-day on Thursdays. After the short afternoon visit, my mom and dad called me in to talk. I searched my brain like a computer on steroids. I tried to think of anything I'd done wrong at school that day or might have done that week. I came up empty. Had the neighbors seen me walking with my friend Jenny and squealed on me?

I walked into the room like a sheep about to be slaughtered. The conversation began rather clumsily. My dad's voice sounded as though it were coming from far off. "How would you like to go live with Uncle Eric and Auntie Ann?"

"W—What?" I stammered. It was the strangest request I had ever heard. I must have looked very dazed, confused, or both. When I came to, they were shaking me. I had fainted! What had I done so wrong they had to ostracize me from the family? I had lived with my family for the past eleven years. We were not rich, but we always seemed to make ends meet. I also reasoned, secretly, that if anyone from the family should go live elsewhere, the most likely choice should be my brother.

First, he was older. Second, he knew his way around town. Third, that would save my parents from paying his transportation to and from school. My head was in a conundrum. All kinds of thoughts were running through my mind, but I knew better than to say anything contrary. My parents firmly believed they knew what was best for their children. They made it emphatically clear that children should always listen to and obey their parents without any backtalk. In other words, children should be seen and not heard. Would you believe that I tried backtalking my dad one time? I received such a backhand slap that I never again entertained the thought of talking back to my parents. You got it? Backtalk equals backhand. The only consoling factor that came from that conversation was when my dad assured me, "We are not talking about right away. We'll wait for when you pass the scholarship exam and you're ready to begin your first term in secondary school."

I sheepishly replied, "Okay, Dad," and ran outside to play with my friends as though nothing happened.

I imagine you're wondering why I mentioned being caught walking with Jenny. During the last two months, Jenny, who lived a few streets from me, started asking me to walk home with her after school. She claimed that some neighborhood boys were always saying mean things to her, so I started walking with her. Not long after, these same neighborhood boys spread false rumors that we were boyfriend and girlfriend.

At first, we both vehemently denied it because it really wasn't true, until one day when I said to her, "Jenny since they're saying that we are boyfriend and girlfriend, I'd like us to become boyfriend and girlfriend for real."

She smiled softly at first then got a big grin on her face and chirped, "Sinclair, I would like that very much." To be honest with you, all I knew was that Jenny was a very good-looking girl. When she smiled, a lovely dimple appeared on each of her cheeks and right in the middle of her chin. That dimpled chin was the most beautiful of all—it just tore my heart to pieces. For that reason alone, I always tried to get her to smile. Apart from that, neither of us had a clue as to what being girlfriend and boyfriend meant. We didn't know the rules or what protocol to follow. Sometimes we stayed after school and did homework together. We played silly games together. We even played this little math love game together that all boyfriends and girlfriends seemed to be playing. You write your name like a fraction, then cancel off matching letters. For example, an E from your last name would cancel out with an E from her last name, etc. These were just silly and goofy games, but we played anything that brought us together, anything that would make us laugh.

Sometimes we met at the local recreation ground and took little walks together. We chanced holding hands when we thought no one was looking, and we ran around on the beach with other friends, swimming, diving, and laughing.

We laughed on and on and on. We giggled at the simplest things, even things that weren't that funny. We were doing all these things very clandestinely. Let me make it clear: we were taking serious chances. It was a serious risk. If our parents got wind of any of these activities, they might beat us or forbid us from seeing each other.

One day when my brother and I were having a brotherly conversation, I worked up the courage to ask him, "Just how do you know when a girl likes you? And if she tells you she likes you, what do you do immediately after she says that to you?"

My brother, simply and profoundly, replied, "Just kiss her!"

I burst out laughing, repeating it, though it sounded rather foolish to me. I couldn't bring myself to ask, "How do you kiss a girl?" If I asked him, and he thought I didn't know, he would laugh at me and tease me unabashedly.

It just so happened that the following Saturday evening, my parents sent me to run an errand close to where Jenny lived. That night, as they say, all the stars aligned. I probably would not have stopped by Jenny's house knowing that her parents would be home. But to my surprise, Jenny was looking out the window.

When she saw me, she called out to me, "Sinclair, it's okay," she said. "My parents went out for a few hours. You can come in for a short time."

I went into the house. Jenny was very excited to show me this new word game called Scrabble. Before she removed the board from the box, I stammered my request, "Would you let me kiss you?"

The box, the game board, and the letters all fell to the floor with a thud. We embraced. Our faces were very close, and our lips were almost touching.

We remained in that position for what seemed like an eternity. All the while, I was more than content, feeling very happy inside because I finally had my first kiss. Suddenly, my whole world came undone when I heard a voice from the twilight zone, "This is not a kiss!" Jenny proceeded to quote from a matinee movie she had seen, one I had not seen. She claimed Alan Ladd said to his girlfriend, "What is a kiss without a sucked tongue?"

My lips parted on cue, like the waters of the Red Sea. I felt her tongue pierce the inner sanctum of my mouth, and I became an instant kisser.

I ran from her house to mine. When I got home, I refused to eat anything. I refused to drink anything. I became jittery.

When morning came, it was Sunday. I made several attempts to brush my teeth very gently, trying not to brush out the taste of her tongue from the night before. But life went on.

CHAPTER 4

It was August vacation, and my friends and I were playing a game of soccer. My friends began shouting out to me, saying they saw my sister approaching the playing field. This was highly unusual. As I ran in her direction, I could see her lips moving, and I could hear her saying, "Daddy wants you to come home now." In the next breath, she continued. "The results of the scholarship exam are in the newspaper. Come home now!"

My entire life changed from the moment I burst through the doors to hear the excitement in my father's voice. "You placed first on the island! My boy placed first on the island!" "Sinclair, my boy, you did it!"

Now he couldn't contain himself. As if he were becoming delirious, he muttered continually, "First place on the island. That's my boy!" My mom joined in, and we had a spontaneous and impromptu family celebration.

I became a local hero. All my friends told me they heard my name being called on our radio station. A few days later, I visited the tailor to get measured for my new school uniform. I was also making arrangements to move to the capital to live with Uncle Eric and Auntie Ann.

In times gone by, the August vacation was always very long. That period is in the height of the dry season in our part of the world, and the powers-that-be thought it the best time to remove the kids from the sweltering heat under the zinc-covered buildings called schools. However, that summer seemed shorter than usual. I had to leave my boyhood friends and my girlfriend. I had to leave the surroundings where I was born and grew up. I knew every nook and cranny of my tiny neighborhood. I was comfortable here. Suddenly, they expected me to leave my comfort zone. I was getting ready to move to the city—a completely different place from my country dwellings.

I would sit down and think for hours at a time. *Will I still be able to play a game of marbles? How about jumping rope with every kid in the neighborhood on a moonlit night? Am I going to become like the town kids—so snooty and sophisticated? Will I be able to keep my old friends? Will I make new friends?*

The first morning of the first semester in my new school greeted me with two distinct and diametrically opposed feelings. I was extremely happy to be in a new school—I had a new haircut and was wearing a brand-new uniform, and I was new. On the other hand, I knew no one. I felt alone, lost, and frightened.

Indeed, everything was new. I had to learn my way around the many buildings that made up my new high school as opposed to the one building that housed my primary school. I also had to learn to navigate to and from Uncle Eric's house, my new abode. In addition, I had to remember the different names of my new teachers and the vast number of new students. But all these things proved to be less intimidating than I thought. In no time, I settled in.

Now, the school exposed me to subjects more complicated than English, arithmetic, history, geography, and hygiene. Suddenly, I was thrust into the big league of academics and introduced to subjects such as English literature, biology, algebra, geometry, and foreign languages—Latin and Spanish.

Spanish class was where I made my first new friend. This boy walked into the classroom three weeks after the semester officially began, and he spoke with a funny accent. As a matter of fact, he had trouble speaking understandable English. We later learned, in a very dramatic and demonstrative way, where he originally came from. He scored a hundred percent on every Spanish test. We soon found out he came from Venezuela. Why on Earth would someone leave Venezuela, a Spanish-speaking country, and land in Grenada, an English-speaking country?

The kids in the class started referring to him as "Amigo," and before long, the entire school population was calling him by his nickname "Amigo." This still didn't clear up the question of why he was attending the school. We eventually learned that his mother, Grace, left Grenada as an eighteen-year-old and traveled to Venezuela to live with her Aunt Venus. What follows is his mom's story.

Life in Grenada was slow, and Grace's aunt was scared her niece would end up pregnant and throw her life away, so she sent for her. Grace had just left elementary school. She was only fifteen years old, tall and skinny with a long neck and a full head of hair. Grace was a beautiful young girl but also sassy and brash. No one could successfully reprimand her; she told them off and gave them a piece of her mind. The older folks in the village would always say, "This girl has a mouth on her. One day it'll get her in a whole heap of trouble."

Everyone called her "Slim," and the people always said—behind her back—that the reason she was so skinny was that her long, thick head of hair was "sucking her dry." Grace became over-joyed with the prospect of leaving Grenada because boredom overtook her after she left primary school. Grace later admitted, "I got out of bed late every morning, did my housework, and once my mom came home from work, I would go gallivanting with my friends."

Her mom saw Grace's life going nowhere, so she badgered her sister to take her. Her aunt complained to Grace's mom in one of her letters, "Life in Venezuela is no bed of roses, you know. And if she is as lazy as you say, Venezuela is no place for her to come and pass the time." In any event, she eventually sent down the ticket and a new outfit for Grace to travel in.

It never crossed Grace's mind that one of the major difficulties would be the language. She knew Venezuela was a Spanish-speaking country, but she thought to herself, my aunt speaks English, and she is living and working there. How difficult could it be for me?

Well, lo and behold—this is a phrase old people always used when they foretold something tragic. Grace was in for a rude awakening.

She landed at Simón Bolívar International Airport, and as she walked into the terminal, her head began to spin. She later confided that she'd never seen so many people before unless it was last lap jump up on Carnival Tuesday night. Then she thought, *everyone around me is speaking gibberish. I can't understand anything that anyone is saying.*

She had never been so happy to see her aunt!

Aunt Venus was tall with a beautiful, well-proportioned body. She looked elegant in a red mid-length dress that hugged her curvaceous hips and accentuated her tight and firm buttocks. The dress highlighted her dark complexion magnificently. She wore a little black hat with dangling gold teardrop earrings. Her black shoes had a modest heel, perfectly matching a black handbag draped over her arm. Aunt Venus was simply poetry in motion. When she saw how glamorous her aunt looked, Grace couldn't help thinking, *I knew my aunt was always a pretty woman. They used to call her Good-Looking Darkie. But today, with just enough makeup on, she looked stunning.*

Aunt Venus spoke to the airport authorities on Grace's behalf in fluent Spanish.

"I was amazed and proud at the same time," said Grace. "I made up my mind from that moment to do all I could to make my auntie proud of me by becoming fluent in Spanish."

Grace immediately began pestering her aunt about learning to speak Spanish. Her aunt told her she should fill her spare time watching soap operas, news, and other shows that sparked her interest. "That way, you get a feel for the pronunciation and the language on the whole."

For the first month, it was very frustrating. Then, ever so slowly, Grace started conversing with her aunt.

One evening, as her aunt came in from work instead of greeting her as she usually did in English, Grace said in very limited and halting Spanish, "Buenos días, señorita. ¿Cómo estás?"

Her auntie dropped her bags, ran to Grace, and gave her a big hug. "That's my girl," she said. From then on, they started saying a few words in Spanish together every day. They began with the Spanish words for colors, household items, casual greetings, and days of the week.

Grace stayed in the house for three whole months before agreeing to go shopping with her auntie. When she finally did, she enjoyed it so much they started going to the markets every Saturday and to the plazas on Thursdays.

Soon she began ordering food from the menus when they went out to eat. Her words were faltering and uneasy at first. Then one day, she went out alone—and she survived! "Little old me," she grudgingly said, "from an unknown little island, Grenada, turning a foreign language into mine. Thanks, Auntie."

When Aunt Venus first came to Venezuela, she worked in people's kitchens. By the time Grace came to live with her, she was a manager for a major corporation. Auntie got a job for Grace as a nanny, working for a rich couple to take care of their baby. It was another golden opportunity for Grace to further improve her Spanish. She said later, "With the child and the television set, I started to relearn the Spanish fundamentals from scratch. This also did wonders to boost my confidence and my self-esteem."

I told you before that her aunt was a good-looking, well-put-together woman. Suffice it to say that the mango didn't fall too far from the tree.

Grace was no longer skinny. She had filled out beautifully. She had developed more-than-adequate breasts and fuller hips, still maintaining her slim waist. Her legs were long, shapely, and strong enough to hold up and accentuate her well-shaped bottom. And she still had her gorgeous head of jet-black hair.

Grace had transformed into a well-sculptured specimen. She was now drop-dead gorgeous.

At first, Auntie helped to groom Grace's sense of fashion. But after two years, Grace became more sophisticated, imaginative, and fashionable in her own right. "I was in control of myself and my destiny," said Grace. "So, when I mentioned to Auntie that I thought I was ready to live on my own, she gave me her full blessing."

Aunt Venus was getting older, and she thought it was time to find a good man and settle down. "Besides," she said, "I don't have to scrape and scrounge to send money down every month to my sister, your mother. Now it's your turn to send money down to help take care of your mother and your siblings."

She happily responded, "I have already started, and I will surely continue."

"Good for you," Auntie replied.

The apartment Grace found was located only a little distance from her aunt's house. But the apartment made her think like a real, bona fide Venezuelan. However, she still longed for home in one form or another.

After gathering her thoughts, she reasoned with herself rather passionately, *I think I am ready to date, but I'm still very wary of dating a Venezuelan.* So, she was relieved when a guy approached her while walking and introduced himself. His name was John and there was something about him and his general demeanor was different. Grace would later learn he also sensed in his spirit that something was different about her. And when he asked for her name, he spoke not in Spanish but English.

CHAPTER 5

After their initial conversation, they exchanged telephone numbers, and she later admitted, "I couldn't wait to get home to receive his phone calls. We would talk long into the night. Sometimes in English, sometimes in Spanish, or sometimes in Spanglish."

One night, she finally agreed to a first date. There was a West Indian party at the Rotary Club, and they decided to attend. When she was all primed and ready, she looked at herself in the mirror and was highly pleased.

Grace opened the door when her date knocked, and they both graciously complimented each other. When they glided onto the dance floor, and she looked around, she whispered to him eagerly, "If there were a Best Dressed Couples Contest, we would win, hands down."

They danced. They laughed. They giggled. They fell in love. She would later reminisce, "I could not wait to get out from under the glare of all those people and be alone with him. Just the both of us, my lover and me."

They left the party to take a walk in the courtyard and sat down very cozily on one of the benches, about to seal their love with their first kiss, when headlights penetrated from a distant car, interrupting the kiss and shattering the mood. After all, they were both in foreign territory. It could have been some gang intruders; it could have been the police; it could have been immigration officers. There was no time for further speculation.

After lighting up the entire compound momentarily, the lights went off without a hitch, but the damage was already done. The couple relaxed as best they could and tried to get back into casual conversation.

After a few quiet seconds had elapsed, the boy said casually to Grace, "As many conversations as we've had, I never asked where you come from originally."

Grace laughed and said shyly, "They call where I'm from the Land of Spice—Grenada. What about you?" she asked. "Where are you from originally?"

He said, nonchalantly, "Panama."

She unconsciously burst out laughing. "I've never met anyone from Panama before, but I have relatives in Panama." Grace then mentioned that her mother always bemoaned the fact that two of her older brothers had gone away to Panama a long time ago to help build the Panama Canal.

Grace looked her friend, John, in the eye and continued. "My mom always mentioned the Panama Canal, but she would become so upset and just kept repeating, 'But they never came back. They never came back.'"

No one knew for sure why they didn't come back, but that never stopped the rumor mills from grinding out possible reasons, based on some facts. The living conditions for West Indian workers in Panama were known to be deplorable, and the work area that needed clearing was a vast jungle filled with deadly snakes. No one knew if one or both of the brothers had been bitten by these venomous snakes. The dilapidated barracks, plus poor hygiene, made all the workers highly susceptible to deadly diseases like pneumonia, typhoid, and even the bubonic plague. The work was difficult and demanded brute strength.

The most dangerous of all the jobs was dynamiting, a task all West Indians were assigned at some point. One of the worst accidents reported occurred during the Panama Canal's construction; the premature explosion of dynamite brought the death of twenty-three West Indian workers and injured forty others. Could the brothers have died in that blast? No one knew for sure.

Dynamite Crew

Many West Indian workers ran headlong into these unknown conditions without even considering the risk factors that might be lurking underneath. There was simply no time for contemplation. The only thing that mattered was promises of wealth and success; many dreamed of finding themselves in a rags-to-riches story. It was all too common—this burning desire to raise oneself and one's family to a more secure financial setting. This was the only reason that drove Grace's uncles to Panama. Ironically, it was the same reason responsible for their mysterious deaths.

Grace explained that her mother never wanted her to travel because she was always afraid her daughter would fail to return home, like her two brothers. However, Grace was always quick to point out to her mother, "Your sister went to Venezuela, and she comes back. So, what's the big deal?"

For some unknown reason, that Panama talk got Grace feeling a little sad. The combination of the interruption from the lights and the sudden injection of Panama into the conversation created a very somber mood, especially when John mentioned his father and uncle dying due to similar circumstances.

Grace gave John a peck on the cheek to try to alleviate his total disappointment, and when he smiled, she was assured they would have another romantic interlude at a later date. She secretly hoped it would be sooner rather than later. Just before John left, she asked haphazardly, "What was your father's name?"

John answered matter-of-factly, "My dad's name was Pluto, and my uncle's name was Uranus."

Grace said her goodbyes and rushed up to her apartment. As if in one swooping motion, she opened the door and immediately picked up the phone.

"Auntie," she said hysterically, "you and my mom are always talking about these two brothers you grew up with—the ones who went to Panama and never came back."

Her aunt must have been asleep because she was slow to answer.

Grace reminded her, "When I was very little, both you and my mom would always try and get my attention whenever the stars would pitch across the sky. Do you remember what you used to tell me?" Grace answered her own question. "You both said to me, 'There go your Uncles Pluto and Uranus. They're going back from whence they came.'"

When Grace was a girl, that phrase always sounded a little funny to her. Even now that she was a grown woman, it still sounded eerie as she repeated it to her aunt.

"Forget about that, 'whence whatever,'" her aunt said, sounding irritated. "Why couldn't this wait till morning?"

"Oh," Grace said with a touch of sarcasm in her voice, "sorry for disturbing you, Miss Auntie. This will only take a minute."

Grace hurriedly and excitedly explained her date and the two names John had mentioned. The next morning, Venus called her sister, Mercury, in Grenada, bright and early. All the details matched. The sisters surmised there were no other children on the island who had the unusual names of Pluto and Uranus. The only thing left was to confirm the last name. Now it was up to Grace to facilitate the next move.

Grace called her boyfriend, John, the next day and thanked him for the wonderful night she'd had. She told him how much she enjoyed their first date and hoped he enjoyed it as much as she had. Grace could hear him stammering over the phone, and he finally bellowed out, "Sure I did . . . I hope we can go out again soon."

That was exactly what she was hoping to hear. She suggested they have dinner with Auntie and her boyfriend. He readily agreed.

Now Auntie, Grace, and Grace's mom began to strategize. Being the older sister, Grace's mom remembered much more than Auntie, so she and Grace did most of the planning over several phone conversations.

They agreed Auntie Venus would choose the restaurant and make the reservations once Grace was able to confirm a date and time with John.

Auntie Venus and her boyfriend, Michael, were the first to arrive at the designated restaurant. Grace and John got there soon after. It was the first time the couples met, so they greeted each other with anxious laughter and vigorous handshakes. They chatted and laughed for a while longer until the concierge finally escorted them to their table.

The four of them sat down and started by ordering drinks. Between waiting for their drinks and making clumsy small talk, Auntie and Grace excused themselves from the table and went to the ladies' room.

Auntie was quick to speak, and she said emphatically to Grace, "I think we should forget this 'Grand Inquisition.' Let bygones be bygones. Your friend is such a fine, good-looking man. I think you should just try to establish the relationship instead of digging up old worms—worms you don't even know exist."

"That's all well and good for you to say, Auntie, but I'm sure you wouldn't want me to date any member of our family—probably a close relative at that."

She considered her niece then gave in. "Oh, all right. We don't know anything for sure, but we're already here, so let's just find out once and for all."

They went back to the table, rejoined the others, and enjoyed their meal, making light conversation and listening to soothing calypso and reggae background music. Auntie's boyfriend turned out to be very comical, so they enjoyed loads of laughs too.

When they finished having dessert, Auntie Venus unflinchingly attacked the subject they were there to discuss. She explained to John the story of her two older brothers going to Panama to help build the Panama Canal but never returning to Grenada.

"So, what was your dad's last name?" she asked, peering into John's eyes.

For a moment, he was taken aback, but with no means to escape the rigidity of the question, he forced a sheepish smile as he answered, "Vincent!"

The full name was not completely out of his trembling lips when Auntie leaped to her feet and started bawling, "God bless my eyesight! You is one of us! You is one of us!"

John was so baffled that his face grew distorted. He was caught on an emotional roller coaster, wanting to cry and wanting to laugh all at the same time. He searched Grace's eyes for answers, but she began sobbing uncontrollably.

Later, Grace summed it up this way: "Was I crying because I was about to lose him as a lover, or was I crying because of my newfound cousin?" She continued as if in a daze, "I couldn't decide then. I still cannot decipher. Auntie Venus welcomed John instantly on behalf of us who were present and on behalf of her sister in Grenada."

John and Grace did the only thing they thought they could and should do—they hugged tightly and promised to be the best cousins ever. Grace, later, intimated he promised to find her a guy as good as him, and he made her promise to find him a woman as beautiful and affable as her.

That night, sleep found no place in her eyes. Grace tossed and turned the entire night, wondering aloud at times if it might have been better to have followed Auntie's prompting to "leave well enough alone."

Morning finally crept in through the crevices of her room, and she smiled. It was still a heavy-hearted smile at the loss of a man who, she reasoned, "would have made me a very happy woman and a contented wife."

To this day, they still talk to each other and laugh at almost being like England's Royal Family, which sometimes allows for marriage within the bloodline. Grace finally quipped, "We jokingly say to each other at times, 'We should have opted for the Royal Vincent Family,' but we did not."

Grace continued hauntingly, "A little again, just a little bit again. We would have been like Lord Melody's calypso 'Shame and Scandal.' This would have been absolutely appropriate for our situation."

She was obviously annoyed and greatly perturbed as she continued to give full vent to her feelings.

"These damn West Indian men. They leave their wives at home, roaming from country to country to make a living. All that is well and good, but they just can't leave the blasted women alone. They end up having children all over the place, and in the long run, it is people like me and John who suffer. That's not good! This is a very bitter pill to swallow. I'm mad and terribly upset about this whole situation."

This was a well-known story that had taken on mythical proportions throughout the length and breadth of the West Indian Islands. The mere fact that the West Indian man was forced to roam caused the normal domestic balances to suffer great and sometimes permanent imbalance. This is how the story was told:

The man leaves his woman or woman and children to work on contract for six to eight months. Sometimes longer. The work is always strenuous, involving manual labor and brute strength. After about three or four months, he comes to grips with his loneliness, coupled with his fabled insatiable sexual appetite. He invariably gets involved with a woman in his new environment. In many instances, these dalliances regrettably lead to the woman becoming pregnant—sometimes unknown to the man.

After his contract ends, the man returns to his home base, leaving the woman and a child behind. The child is left in a faraway place carrying either the mother's or the father's last name. But the chances of the parents ever seeing each other again are extremely remote.

In the meantime, this woman he left at home finds herself in the same cantankerous situation. She reasons that she too is affected by loneliness and the same fabled insatiable sexual appetite to which her man falls victim. She has an affair, which sometimes leads to her becoming pregnant.

The man returns home and is duped into believing he fathered the child before he left to fulfill his contract.

Both people are none the wiser. He does not tell her about the child he fathered while he was away, and she does not tell him about the child he thinks he fathered. Therein lies the confusion. Years go by, the children grow, and they meet in a neutral country through their travels. They fall in love but are unable to consummate their love when fate reveals the truth about their true backgrounds. Therein lies the shame.

This pathetic story of lies, drama, and intrigue had been the gruesome downfall of many West Indian lives. This story was so poignant that it was now an integral part of West Indian culture and folklore. The story had also been translated into a popular song to establish forever the woes that had befallen many generations of West Indian men and women—all because the West Indian man was forced to find employment far away from home.

The calypso song Grace referred to was called "Shame and Scandal in the Family." The calypso weaved the story of a young man's desire to get married. He fell in love with a beautiful young woman and brought her home to receive his father's blessing.

The son was astonished when his father gave him the sad, unexpected news: the young woman he wanted to marry was his sister.

"But how can that be?" the young man questioned. Her name had never been mentioned in the household, and he had no inclination about this new and baffling information.

He was also further prompted by his father to withhold this news from his mother. Why? Because she was totally unaware of the young woman's existence. In other words, his dad's wife—the boy's mother—was not the young woman's mother.

The young man was very distraught. He was skeptical and stopped dating for almost a year before he fell in love again.

He brought this young woman for his father's approval. He was utterly amazed when his father gave him the same response. "This girl," he insisted, "is your sister, but your mother does not know."

The young man, desperate and despondent, went out of his mind. He could not fathom the level or depth of this jinx. Twice jilted, he thought long and hard about abandoning the idea of marriage. He stopped dating completely.

In time, the young man easily replaced love for women with the love of alcohol. His life was spiraling out of control when he was propped up by one of the nurses at his rehabilitation center.

It took all of the nerves he could muster to think of marriage. This time, though, he brought this fiancé to his mother and not his father.

He was pleasantly surprised when he instantly received his mother's blessing.

He tried to tell his mother about his father's reasoning for refusing to give him his blessings.

The mother coyly confided in him that his father was not his father, but his father did not know.

Could you imagine the young man's dilemma? Finally faced with some delayed truths, half-baked lies, drama, and innuendos, tremors shook his fundamental beliefs.

This was the same intrigue that Grace was experiencing. She was bitter and distraught. She wished, in all sincerity, the ground she stood on would open and swallow her up. For a long time, she thought she might be better off dead than alive.

But in the end, Grace kept her sanity.

She went through a self-imposed period of grieving. She found it very difficult to sleep, tormented for a while with terrible nightmares. After many sleepless nights, she ambled to work in a daze, not knowing if she would make it.

In time, she was able to testify to the power of prayer and effortless meditation. This period of suffering ended when she met and fell in love with a handsome Venezuelan man. She learned her lesson well. She reasoned that if she chose a native Venezuelan to be in her life, she would lessen her chances of falling in love with an unknown relative again.

Her Aunt Venus took immediate charge of the wedding preparations. The first concern was to explore the possibility of getting a visa to accommodate Grace's mom traveling from Grenada to Venezuela in time for the wedding.

Nine months after her marriage, Grace gave birth to her only son. Twelve years later, she sent him back to Grenada to live with his aging grandmother, believing it would be the ideal environment for him to grow up in.

This was the young man who turned up at my high school with the funny accent. The same young man everyone called "Amigo."

CHAPTER 6

The semester had started for me in September, and before I knew it, we were preparing for our first major exams before the Christmas break. Though I was smart—remember, I placed first in the island's exam—I was never acutely aware of it. And for the first time in my life, school became a war zone. This guy came up to my face one time and, after introducing himself, lambasted me. "You are the one they say is the brightest kid on the island? Well," he said sarcastically, "I'm going to cut you down just as small as Pretender."

I immediately recognized the reference to one of Mighty Sparrow's calypso songs, so I sheepishly and nonchalantly replied, "Ten to One is Murder."

A gentle smile replaced his gruff and gritty countenance, and he said, "You know calypso too?"

Although stunned by our shared interest, he kept me at a distance for a time. James seemed like an obnoxious and aggressive boy. It appeared to me that he was carrying the world on his shoulders, but he didn't want anyone to know. He wanted everyone to like him, and if you didn't like him, he would have utter contempt for you.

I assessed him from afar during the first few weeks after our encounter. He struck me as being a needy person, constantly seeking attention.

James walked around the classroom with a bravado that signified he had been at the school for years and not weeks. His chest was puffed out as though everyone should be subservient to him.

The morning James approached me, I could feel his contempt for me. When he spoke, his upper lip curled in disdain.

I refused to play his games. I stood up to him in a fashion he was unaccustomed to, proving I was in his league.

We started speaking to each other from that moment, and he realized we shared other similar untoward circumstances. His parents had also left him in the care of someone else, his grandma. What a sick joke!

James and I handled that traumatic event differently. But the shared circumstance was a major reason our friendship blossomed.

Sometimes, we would sit for hours discussing and arguing who we thought were the greatest calypsonians from a very crowded field: Mighty Sparrow, Lord Kitchener, The Duke, Chalkdust, Super Blue, 'Soso,' Beckett, Ajamu, The Tradewinds, Fab Five, David Rudder, and others.

We examined the lyrics of these masters, noting their timely local political commentaries. We also lamented over not studying them in the same way we had to slave over the lyrics and verses of Shakespeare, Percy Bysshe Shelley, and even Chaucer. Do you remember Chaucer's *Canterbury Tales*? The collection of twenty-four stories ran to over 17,000 lines, and the disturbing part was these lines were written in a type of Middle English. The tales came with an elaborate vocabulary we needed to learn in order to read them.

Can you believe that? The West Indian language, which was in calypsos, we were discouraged from listening to, much less memorizing the lines. Be that as it may, we were still die-hard calypso fanatics.

I will never forget the first time we heard what we called a *classic*. We took the record to my friend's house, and we played that song over and over again. Later that evening, one of our friends joked, "You guys need to give this sparrow something to eat!" He continued with all the cleverness he could muster, "He has been singing and singing all morning without a break."

"Well," my friend quipped, "we should be so lucky because he's only a little sparrow. He don't eat too much."

We ended up on the floor, dying with uproarious laughter. You know what West Indians mean when they say, "You laugh 'til yuh belly buss?" That was the kind of laughter we succumbed to.

The name of the classic calypso I'm referring to is "Federation." The name of the calypsonian is Mighty Sparrow.

The song dealt with the gallant effort to unify the West Indian Islands under one umbrella or Federation and its later demise. The idea of a federated West Indies appealed to all my friends and me because we knew very little of these islands in our hemisphere. We were ecstatic as we thought a federation would be the ideal vehicle to expose us to learning and caring more about ourselves and our sister islands, but that was not to be. The Federation failed.

We listened to this calypso over and over again because we were intrigued with how the calypso chronicled the events of the Federation from its glorious and hopeful beginnings to its woeful and tragic end. The song vehemently blamed Jamaica, and rightfully so, for the breaking up of the Federation.

My friends and I were devastated by the break-up of the Federation; we thought our dreams were shattered.

Would there be no chance to learn more about ourselves and our sister islands? Should we see this as a total abandonment to learning more about our West Indian culture and heritage?

It, therefore, came as a complete surprise and a colossal reversal when the school heralded a change to its curriculum.

A History of the West Indies' textbook replaced the history of Britain and its colonies. The World Geography textbook gave way to a more

Caribbean-oriented text, and new upcoming West Indian authors now stood alongside Shakespeare. Everything was going fine just how we wanted it when we were caught unawares.

An Englishman replaced our local English Literature teacher.

We later found out our former teacher had gone to England on an exchange program. The students were displeased, but we settled for Mr. Ishawood from Birmingham, England.

He was desperate to fit in; he shopped at the local markets, ate local foods, and dated local women.

In one of our class sessions, we read a story titled "The Ravages of Slavery." Then, after a few weeks had passed, Mr. Ishawood gave us a homework assignment that none of us expected.

The assignment read as follows: *Are West Indian people still feeling the ravages from the aftermath of slavery? Discuss. Make sure to support your arguments with writings, poetry, and/or song. Talk to your parents and grandparents to try and make your findings as authentic as possible.*

We had four weeks to hand in our papers.

He wanted us to break up into groups of four on our own, but if we had problems, our teacher promised to do it randomly. No one wanted it to be done randomly, so we hurried to form groups among our friends.

My group consisted of Carl, Isaac, my best friend, James, and me.

We spent hours in the library, and we read our West Indian history books more avidly than ever. Those of us on the football team skipped a few practice sessions to meet up in the library for more discussions.

We spoke to our parents and grandparents, but they either knew very little or were unwilling to tell us much.

However, they were very adamant about one thing: they were all willing to spend their last dollar sending us to school to "stay far away from working lands." They all wanted us to strive to become doctors or lawyers or be employed at a job that demanded we wear a jacket and tie.

The only real thought they had about slavery was its bitter connection to working the sugarcane fields in the sweltering sun or torrential rains.

Week three came, and we were at an impasse with our homework assignment. The problem was trying to compile the information into a coherent and cohesive whole.

We were frustrated. The project was draining us. We were forced to deal with our history head-on and in a practical way. We knew about slavery, but we had only read it as a story that happened to our people once upon a time. We were not consciously aware of the importance attached to the period of slavery. In our minds, we only thought of it as history, the study of past events. We also reasoned that we were taking an English literature class—not a history class. We had nearly given up on the project when James hastily summoned a meeting with the group.

He intimated that we should meet at his house to listen to a calypso.

"What?" We all cried in unison. Nevertheless, we were excited because we all loved calypso music. We danced to the fast, pulsating beat. We sometimes sang its risqué lyrics. Most of all, we loved the picong, the light comical banter, usually at someone else's expense. It is how West Indians tease, heckle, and mock each other in a friendly manner. Calypsonians were masters in the art of picong.

We settled down in the living room of James's house, not knowing what to expect. All we knew was that we were itching to hear this new calypso by Mighty Sparrow, the calypso king of the world. We felt we were in for a treat.

The name of the calypso was "Slave." The calypso began to play, and we immediately sensed that the tempo of the music was different from what usually ascribed calypso music. The rhythm was deliberately slower and more urgent.

The format of the song was also different. The calypso format usually had a verse and a chorus, followed by a lengthy musical interlude before the next verse continued. But "Slave" had only a brief musical interlude before the next verse continued. I felt like I was listening to an uninterrupted story, and this story was particularly gripping.

Our heads moved in unison toward the record player. We were captivated and immersed in the story. We felt as though we were being carried away to the shores of Africa by the ships of the Middle Passage then transported onto the auction blocks in the West Indies.

The lyrics spoke of the capture of masses of Black people, forced to work on the sugar plantations in the West Indies.

The verses told of the anguish of leaving home to face the unknown. The chorus kept on drumming the mantra: "I'm dying. I just want to be free."

When the song was finished, the four of us sat around the table stupefied and dumbfounded for minutes.

We finally had the information we needed to finish our assignment. We used this calypso as the skeleton for our presentation. From then on, it was easy to add the meat of our argument onto these bones.

We received an A for our exposé.

I must say here that James and I had many heated arguments about calypsos and calypsonians. After all, he was a Lord Kitchener fan while I was 100 percent in Mighty Sparrow's camp. These debates grew most fervent around Trinidad's Carnival time.

Carnival holds a sacred spot on every Trinidadian's calendar and is one of the biggest street celebrations. It's an annual event held on the Monday and Tuesday before Ash Wednesday.

Carnival originated as a pagan festival in ancient Egypt and was subsequently celebrated by the Greeks and Romans. It's said the festival was brought to Trinidad by French settlers, who carried the Fat Tuesday tradition with them to the islands in the eighteenth century.

On these two days, people dress up to mimic comical characters and masquerade bands portray ancient and modern civilizations. These costumed bands parade through the streets as they vie for prizes for the most authentic depictions.

It would be impossible for these bands to parade through the streets without the accompaniment of music. The indigenous music of Trinidad is called calypso music, and the musicians are called calypsonians. These songs relay the local happenings of the day told in very creative and humorous lyrics.

During the parade, the calypso, sung the most by the masquerading bands, is adjudged the winner of the road march.

There can be no Carnival without calypso, and there can be no calypso without Carnival.

However, in the case of Mighty Sparrow's calypso "Slave," we both stood in awe. We recognized genius when we saw it. "De man take a whole history book and put it in one song? Dat is man!" my friend said, the words rattling off his tongue in an excited manner.

CHAPTER 7

Because I came from the country and was now living in town, I took special care to pronounce my words properly and not "talk bad" as I was accustomed to doing.

I knew if I was caught talking like a country bookie, I would be ridiculed, scorned, teased, and laughed at by my peers. So, I was extra careful, but every now and again, James would slip up and use some country expressions when we were alone. One day, I confronted him point-blank, "Where you really from?"

He smiled widely and asked, "Why?"

"Because," I said, "every so often when we're together, you sound like you came from the country too."

He prefaced his answer by saying, "We're friends, so anything I say remains here."

"Right on," I replied, borrowing a phrase I'd heard a few days earlier from one of the students returning from a holiday in the United States.

"The truth is," he said, looking around to make sure no one else was within hearing distance, "I was born in the city. But when I was five years old, my parents took me to live in the country with my dad's mom."

"Yeah?" I heard myself saying, "Why did they have to do that?"

"Because," he continued, "they decided to go to England."

"And leave you here?" The words just jumped out of my mouth. I couldn't fathom how a family could leave their child and go to England. It was just so far away and so unknown. How could they leave all that sun and all that freedom?

Now he was getting agitated. "Putting all jokes aside, you know what does fret me? Is when ah see all these white people coming here and walking about half-naked with no shoes on their feet and enjoying we little island, and we leaving de sun to go in de cold." He stopped for a moment to catch his breath. "Something ain't right." He started shaking his head from left to right. "Dat doh make no sense."

He became very emotional. I had never seen him like that before, so I was determined to say something on his parents' behalf. Measuring my words with controlled speed, I began, "You know things are kind of hard here for parents. There aren't too many jobs, and even if they're working, their salary is not that great, so they're just trying something."

"Yeah!" he snapped. "But not at my expense. They leave me here with de ole woman, and as far as I hear, they have a brand-new family up there. You think they have time for me and Grandmother?"

I calmly said to him, "You can't say dat, man. You in secondary school, and you always have English money in your pocket and English clothes on your back."

"Let me tell you something." He was now very adamant. "My parents were just lucky that I passed the scholarship exams, so they don't have to pay my school tuition. When they send money for me, you change a one-pound note in the bank and get four dollars and eighty cents. So, they could afford to send me two hundred pounds for a year, and all the fellas would think I'm a big shot. That's the only thing."

The other students started milling around, so we got back into character as we greeted our other buddies in idle chatter.

This conversation had such a powerful impact on me that I ran home and asked my uncle if I could visit my parents over the weekend. Suddenly, I began to feel like my friend—my parents lived on the same island as me, but I never saw them. My uncle was too busy to drive me up that weekend, so I got on the bus for the two-and-a-half-hour ride.

The first words out of my dad's mouth on my first self-made visit were, "God works in mysterious ways, His wonders to perform." He kept going on and on. "You saved us a trip because we were coming to tell you the good news."

"What's the good news, Dad?" I asked.

He continued, oblivious, "The little shop is not doing too well lately, so your mom and I have decided that we should give England a try."

"What does that mean?" I persisted.

"This means," he said, "we will be traveling to England to try our luck."

I could not believe my ears! I sat totally dumbfounded. Instead of asking my dad the questions I had in my mind, I started asking myself so many questions all at the same time. My head became so muddled I felt as though I was beginning to lose my mind. My brain started playing tricks on me. Pictures raced through my mind, images from all the English stories I'd read in the English Royal Reader books. I could envision myself as "Solomon Slow" missing his bus to school; I saw the English landscapes like Trafalgar Square and Piccadilly Circus; I could see myself visiting England's revered Old Trafford Cricket Ground; I even saw myself visiting Buckingham Palace. Would I be lucky enough to get a chance encounter with the Queen?

I knew so much about England, so much more than I knew about my little island. I can honestly say that at the time I knew very little about the other islands that made up the West Indies. Instead, England's history was my history. I was on a first-name basis with all her heroes: Walter Rodney,

Francis Drake, Walter Raleigh, and Winston Churchill, to name a few. I was living in Grenada, but I knew and cared more about England as the Mother Country. The teachers drilled it into us every day without fail. I was programmed enough to long for the privilege of stepping onto British soil. I am willing to wager all my money that I had a very contented smile on my face during my astral travel.

Then, I was rudely awakened out of all these wild, vivid, and crazy possibilities by my father's booming voice, shattering my mind with all its illusions.

"Your mom and I think it's best to leave you here to finish your studies, and we will take the other children with us."

It was like I was hearing him in slow motion.

"Father," I heard myself blurting out. "Father, are there no schools in England that I can attend? After all, England is supposed to be the seat of learning and the seat of civilization. This will be the ideal place for me to do my studies. Why can't I go to England with the rest of the family?"

He mumbled something under his breath, but I knew his mind was already made up.

I got up, feeling extremely disgusted. I said my goodbyes then and there and prepared for the journey back to school the next morning.

In the following months, I immersed myself in my books like never before, and I became completely involved in as many sporting activities as were available to me: cricket, football, track and field, and tennis. I had boundless energy. As a matter of fact, I went on to become captain of the school's cricket and football teams. For the next three years, my friend and I also played cricket for the island. Playing for the national team at sixteen years old, I became a phenom; I could be likened to an unstoppable freight train. I was an untamed horse without a bridle.

Would you believe that from the time my entire family left for England, I never heard from them again? I don't know whether my dad was sending money to Uncle Eric or not, but Uncle Eric and Aunt Ann gave me everything I wanted. In time, I slowly began to see them as my parents. They, in turn, treated me as their only son.

Time passed in a blur of activity, and I did nothing to slow it. I relished the pace, the attention, and especially the way it dulled the pain of my abandonment. Two years later, the proverbial burning of the midnight oil paid off. I stood on the stage of my school's auditorium, in front of the who's who of the island. In addition to my adoptive parents, my school's principal, the governor, and the chief minister were in attendance.

I was presented the honor and distinction of Island Scholar, a prestigious award given to the student who had the best overall grade among all eligible students who sat the final exams in high school. I was on cloud nine. I was being praised by my peers and honored by the elders. I had achieved a truly remarkable feat.

My biological parents were not there to share my joy. My brother and sisters were nowhere in sight. Beneath my joyful exterior, I was distraught. From that night forward, I renounced my biological parents and promoted Uncle Eric and Aunt Ann to the distinguished role as my mom and dad.

That summer, my friend, James, left to join his parents in England. I left soon after to continue my studies at the prestigious University of the West Indies at Mona, Jamaica, West Indies. For the next few years, I completed both my graduate and postgraduate degrees at U.W.I.

I also found time to play first-class cricket for the West Indies as a batsman. I became a star batsman, a prolific scorer, and a terrific close to the bat fieldsman. I played throughout the West Indian Islands and toured with the team to Australia and India.

Then, the moment I had secretly been hoping for finally came: we were going to tour England.

When the team toured England, I was sure I would be reunited with my family. As a star batsman, my name and picture were plastered on every English newspaper, every television screen, and every radio broadcast all over England and the West Indies.

But not even these fires were hot enough to smoke out my relatives from their holes. Not my father, not my mother, not my older brother, not even my younger sisters. Not one relative contacted me.

This was such a shock. I couldn't understand the reasoning. The experience wreaked havoc on my mind, my body, and my soul. I took it so seriously that I became a nervous wreck, and it eventually took its toll on my cricketing form. So, before I was dropped from the team, I graciously retired.

CHAPTER 8

My retirement sent shockwaves through the cricketing world. My teammates couldn't understand it. Sportswriters and commentators tried but could not put a handle on it. After I retired from cricket, I was offered a professor's position at the University of the West Indies, at the Cave Hill campus in Barbados. I accepted.

My studies behind me, and my cricketing career ended, I started playing the romantic field like I never had before. I had women by the boatload. It was easy for me to attract the most beautiful and intelligent women from all the islands I visited. After all, I had been dubbed as one of the world's most eligible bachelors. Sinclair, good-looking, talented, and smart, I busied myself with as many girlfriends as I could possibly have all at the same time. I had an Indian girlfriend in Grenada, a Syrian and a Chinese girlfriend in Trinidad, a Portuguese girlfriend in St. Vincent, a mulatto girlfriend in St. Lucia, and a Dougal girlfriend in Guyana.

You might be wondering how I could find all these different nationalities in the Caribbean. You might also be thinking that they were probably just visiting these islands for an extended period when I met them. No. They were all born in their respective islands. YES, THEY WERE ALL ISLAND GIRLS. But how could this be? Let me try and jog your memory.

In 1492, Christopher Columbus, an Italian seafarer, found favor with King Ferdinand and Queen Isabella of Spain. In an effort to begin building an empire, they sponsored Columbus's first voyage to hopefully discover a new world. This was the beginning of European speculation that would eventually span the Caribbean Sea. By the end of the nineteenth century, the Caribbean Islands had sprinklings of all the European races. This can be seen as the equivalent of today's space experiment started by Russia in the 1960s. After Russian space exploration began, America quickly followed suit. In the 1990s, almost every major nation in the world had a stake in the hopeful idea of conquering a piece of the stratosphere.

Similarly, when humankind began to explore Earth, it was Spain who was credited as the first world explorer. Soon after, she was joined by her European rivals: Portugal, England, and France. In order to establish ownership and sovereignty, each of these European countries brought people, livestock, and other necessities to work the lands and to get acclimated. The new and unfamiliar climate and terrain proved to be very unsuitable for the white indentured servants. The Europeans, therefore, remedied this by importing more suitable workers from Africa, India, China, Syria, and elsewhere to populate the regions and to also increase the food supply chain.

The Caribbean Islands thus became inhabited with people from almost every part of the globe. This phenomenon gave rise to a complex variety of human crossbreeding never seen before. It was regarded as an anomaly in genetic mutation. For example, the child of a white man and a black woman was called a *mulatto*. The child of a black man and an Indian woman was called a *dougla*. And so on, and so on. Strange as it may seem, I did not have to leave the Caribbean to find any of the women of different races I dated. They were all well represented in this melting pot of humanity. I was presented with a smorgasbord of women, and I helped myself.

After about two years, this extravagant, whimsical lifestyle of all-night partying and incessant womanizing began to lose its appeal. Around the same time, I met and fell in love with a young, attractive, and intelligent woman. God had smiled on me at the right time.

I gave all my attention to "My Sweetness," "My Caribbean Queen," as I'd nicknamed her. Her name was Julie, and she was indeed "sweet, sweet, sweet like a Julie mango." Her copper complexion and hazel eyes told you from the outset that she was of mixed parentage. Her mother was born in Barbados to English parents. Her father was a great-grandson of a Barbadian slave.

She was a slender woman but still had the right amount of meat on her bones—enough for her man to hold on to. In stocking feet, she was about 5'4", but she was instantly transformed to 5'8" in her high heels. I guessed her measurements to be about 38-26-36. Her smile was infectious, and her walk—yes, her walk. The way she moved. Her hips swayed with the rhythmic precision of an old grandfather clock's pendulum. Her walk endeared both men and women to stop and take a second look. The guys hanging out on the corner compared the movement of her derriere to the sound of a windshield wiper in motion: *swish-swoosh, swish-swoosh*. But she wasn't all looks. Julie was kindhearted and very generous. She always had a pleasant smile for everyone she met, and in turn, everyone showered her with love. Even the rough and rugged guys that controlled the corner were very protective of her. To state it simply, anyone who knew her couldn't help but love her. Can you begin to see my dilemma?

Julie was extremely cautious at the beginning of our relationship. She limited the extent of our meetings to phone conversations and our "bumping into each other" encounters. This soon gave way, under my insistence, to real dating. I was able to dispel her doubts and her misgivings about me and my past. As for me, I was scared to lose this chance of a lifetime. I was convinced deep in my soul that she was the 'One.' I was determined to make her my wife. I said to myself, "Sinclair, please don't mess this one up!"

Now you have an idea as to why the relationship started getting serious rather quickly. Did I mention she was a lawyer? When we started talking about marriage, she became very melancholy.

"In order for us to get married," she intoned, "We both need to get the blessing of my parents."

I replied quickly, "I've been wanting to meet your parents for some time. Just give me the directions, and we'll go visit them right now."

She stopped walking, placed her hand in mine, and simply said, "My parents don't live here in Barbados."

"Not again," I heard myself saying in a disgusted tone. "Don't tell me your parents are living in England too?"

She became lighthearted and said, "Don't you know that they call Barbados 'Little England'?"

"Why would they leave England and go to England?"

I must confess I'd never heard about the nickname before, so now I was more curious than ever. I said under my breath, "These damn West Indians. Anywhere in the world you go, you're sure to find a West Indian living there." So, I gathered up my senses, this time addressing her directly. "Where in the world are your parents living?"

She gave me three guesses. I was so programmed that I answered it must be either Canada or America; and, despite what she'd told me a minute ago, I still guessed England.

When she said, "No," I almost shriveled up. But she was now in a playful mood, and she started teasing and taunting me.

"Mr. Professor Sinclair," she said, "do you think the world is that small—England, Canada, and America?" She was on a roll. "You say cricket took you all around the world. Well, your world is too small for me, pal," she chided.

I was now becoming flustered. I threw my hands in the air as we do in the game of cricket to ask for a decision. Without missing a beat, she shouted like an umpire with her index finger pointing upward, "You're out!"

She was so funny that I just embraced her, and we both broke into hysterical laughter.

"You're so funny," I said.

Then, she added with all the sassiness in the world, "And smart too."

After we calmed down, she proclaimed, "My parents are living in Guyana." She continued with her bragging rights, "You ever heard about Cheddi Jagan and Forbes Burnham?"

"Guyana?" I questioned. I continued as if in awe, "I've always heard about people leaving Grenada to go to Trinidad. I've heard about people leaving St. Lucia to go to Barbados. I've even heard about people leaving Dominica to go to Antigua or people leaving Nevis/St. Kitts for the Virgin Islands. But Barbados to Guyana? What's the connection?"

"No special connection other than the usual one," she continued. "The only connection between all the islands you mentioned, including Barbados and Guyana, is this—people looking to find work, more money to help and improve their family's status in life back home."

She turned her head sideways and squinted like she was searching for something, then she said in a gleeful tone, "Dignity. That is the only connection."

Her mood changed quickly, and in a very slow and solemn tone, she indicated, "They are all searching for a higher ground.

"No, correction," she whispered hesitantly, "we are all searching. Look at us. You moved from Grenada to Jamaica to Barbados. I moved from Barbados to Guyana back to Barbados. Moving around seems to be our destiny."

We started to have serious conversations regarding our trip to Guyana to visit her parents. It took us a little longer than we anticipated to coordinate our vacation times. Once this was done, we bought our tickets and were on our way to see her parents. Suddenly, hidden beneath the excitement of this incredible trip was the reality that the central purpose was to ask her parents for her hand in marriage.

We boarded the BWIA airplane, and within two hours, the air hostess made us aware that we were about to touch down at the Timehri Airport.

My girlfriend was so excited about the chance to show me around

Guyana. Up to that time, I was still unaware that she had spent lots of time in Guyana with her parents until she went back to the University of the West Indies Cave Hill Campus in Barbados to complete her studies.

As I said before, I met her in Barbados, replete with her sexy Bajan accent, so I assumed all along that she was Bajan. Well, let me stop here because, in truth and fact, she was born a Barbadian but lived in dual homes in Barbados and Guyana.

We landed at Timehri Airport, and Julie was as giddy and excited as a hallucinating kangaroo. She knew I had played cricket at the Bourda Cricket Ground, one of the best known in the Caribbean. She also deduced I was at least familiar with Georgetown, the capital city of Guyana. Nonetheless, she was smiling from ear to ear as she strutted like a peacock. She was riding on thin air. After all, this was her time to show me around her town, like only she could.

We jumped in a cab and drove down the East Bank Road to Georgetown. As we drove, she took out a pen from her bag and turned it into a pretend microphone. She was now, for all intents and purposes, my official tour guide.

"If you look to the left," she said, laughing, "you'll see the army livestock area, which houses all the livestock to feed the thousands of soldiers in the army."

Then we passed the distilleries where the rums were purified, including Guyana's favorite, El Dorado Rum.

Julie gasped. "Ah! The Floating Bridge."

I was amazed to see the bridge magnificently suspended in midair. She had every right to be as excited as she was, and she got me excited as well. A note of interest: the Demerara Harbour Bridge is the world's longest floating bridge at 1.5 miles long.

Next, Julie pointed out the Demerara Distillers Limited, the home of Banks Beer. I thought this was odd and immediately drew another parallel between Guyana and Barbados for making beers with the same name.

As we drove through the city, she pointed out the police and army headquarters then the seawall. She was anxious to explain that the seawall was built to keep out the waters from the Atlantic Ocean. The seawall is four miles long, five feet wide, and five feet high; but the most important aspect of the wall is bringing the community together. There is nothing to compare to the Sunday "lime," where boy meets girl, resulting in endless possibilities. Another important aspect of the wall, according to my guide, was the launching pad for the kites that covered the skies during the Easter season. My official guide, my girlfriend, thought the wall was the most practical and the most used facility in her beloved Georgetown. We enjoyed some local snacks like chicken foot and coconut water while we took a stroll on the seawall, then we stopped for lunch. Of all the restaurants we could have chosen, we chose to eat at the Coal Pot. Enough said.

We got back into the cab for the hour-and-a-half ride to the ferry. On our way, Julie continued to point out more of the notable sites along the route. She pointed out the University of Guyana buildings, and she was ecstatic when we passed the official building of the former beloved Prime Minister of Guyana, the Honorable Forbes Burnham. We continued along the East Coast Road onto the ferry to cross the Demerara River. We got off the ferry and drove onto the longest continuous straight road in the Caribbean. We drove to the Albion Estate, where Julie's father worked. Because of his position as a manager, he and his wife lived in one of the estate houses, which was part of the overall compound. We arrived at the estate house after a long but interesting and eventful day.

But when her dad finally answered the door, I was more exhilarated than exhausted. We exchanged pleasantries then sat down to a very sumptuous dinner. The menu included, but was not limited to, Guyana's cook-up rice, Bajan boned flying fish, and cuckoo. The appetizer was St. Lucia's national dish, fig, and saltfish, which we washed down with mugs of

Trinidad's grapefruit juice. After dinner, guess what? Dessert was black cake from Grenada and Blue Mountain Coffee from Jamaica.

I was stuffed. We were all stuffed. The mood was very relaxed, and the conversation was light and civil. After dinner, Julie's dad and I retired to the living room while Julie and her mom went to the kitchen to help the maid with the cleaning up. We were talking and laughing, just her dad and I, when I was suddenly jolted back to reality. It dawned on me that my girlfriend and I had made this visit for one purpose. I wondered when the right time would be to broach the subject of my desire to marry his daughter.

I continued to search my mind. I thought maybe I should wait until the four of us were together. Then I reconsidered; maybe I should address it with him now. My thoughts were shifting like quicksand. I became unglued. I hurriedly excused myself and went to the bathroom for what seemed like an eternity. However, when I checked my watch, I had only remained in the bathroom for all of five minutes.

I questioned myself. I cross-examined the timing of my strategy. This whole ordeal became more stressful when I realized my girlfriend and I had not planned anything. All she told me was we must visit her parents to tell them about our plans to get married. As a matter of fact, she was more than emphatic when she stated, "We must get their blessings, or else there can be no marriage." I'd hopped on the airplane with her, and here we were—or should I say, there I was face to face with the father. I was in a total state of unease.

The ice broke when Julie's father told me rather casually that he had been a faithful and ardent follower of my life. *Strange*, I thought, but I hastily realized that my name and my picture graced many of the islands' newspapers that had followed my academic and cricketing careers. He was able to recite my academic achievements, and he proved to be a lifetime fan when he was able to talk glibly about my cricketing prowess. He was overly generous with his compliments and stated it was an added pleasure for him to get to know me. He went on to say it was a mighty privilege for him and his wife "to break bread" with me, as he put it.

A broad smile lit my face, as I thought this was my big break. Here was my chance. I even quoted in my mind the part of the marriage vow that says, "Speak now or forever hold your peace." I immediately followed the cue then and there, clumsily asking for permission to marry his daughter.

Reading this part about permission, you may be dying with laughter. I can hear you saying I didn't need to ask permission—I only needed to ask his daughter. After all, I didn't want to marry the father; I wanted to marry the daughter. True, but the daughter I wanted to marry was his daughter. So, before you go on and on, let me remind you how it was "back in the day."

The man was required to write a very formal letter to his girlfriend's father, asking for his daughter's hand in marriage. Here is a snippet from an actual letter to give you an idea as to the protocol expected of a West Indian wedding:

10 Hard Road Drive
Bridgetown, Barbados

March 10, 1960

Mr. Harold Smith
14 Barron Street
Guyana

Dear Sir,
Here is hoping this letter reaches you safe as it left me. I am writing to ask you for your daughter's hand in marriage. I am anxiously awaiting your pleasant reply with bated breath.

Yours Sincerely,
Moses Cumberbatch

Before her father answered me, he called out to his wife and daughter to join us for a toast. The ladies walked into the living room, looking like wild deer caught in the glare of a massive searchlight. My girlfriend came in with total wonderment. She figured out that I was waiting for her and her mother to be present before I said anything to her father. The mother came in with a questionable look about the toast. "Why are we toasting? What's the occasion?"

To complicate the situation, and to make matters worse through the chaos, I got down on one knee. I took a tiny box out of my pocket. And holding Julie's left hand, I proposed to her in front of her parents with all the dramatics I could summon.

She said yes in a shrill voice and broke down into uncontrollable tears. She kept on crying. There was no stopping her. She buried her head into my shoulder, and the tears seeped through the thin material of my short-sleeve shirt. These were real tears. She kept on crying until her mom pried her away from me and was finally able to quiet her down after about thirty minutes of non-stop crying.

It was good fortune that the parents used their conservative sensibilities and had prepared two separate bedrooms ahead of time. After all, we were not yet married, and biblical scripture taught that we could not sleep together. In retrospect, I was happy they made that decision because that night I slept like a baby.

I woke up the next morning thinking to myself, *wow, I really did it!* The truth is I did not make any preparations, nor did I have any intention of proposing that night. It was all an accident. I had passed by the jewelry store the evening we were leaving Barbados to pick up a watchband to replace my old one. The jeweler said to me, "I didn't expect you today, but the ring is ready, so you might as well pick it up now."

Without giving it a second thought, I reacted. "Sure, why not?" I put the ring in my pocket with the intention of hiding it in a corner of my traveling suitcase where Julie would never see it. Then I realized, though, that sometimes travelers arrive at their destinations without their suitcases. On second thought, I decided the ring was safest in my pocket. That was how everything worked out.

When the four of us sat down to breakfast the next morning, that old favorite scripture reading in Psalms shone through in all its glory, *"Weeping may endure for a night, but joy cometh in the morning."* We thanked Julie's parents for a wonderful time and for going out of their way to show us, especially me, such a good time. We said our goodbyes, and we were chauffeured to the airport by one of her dad's company cars. I continued to let Julie know how pleased I was with the exquisite treatment her parents meted out to me. I told her I was head over heels for her parents.

"I can't wait for them to be, officially, my parents-in-law," I said, kissing her forehead. We were all lovey-dovey, laughing and teasing each other until it came time to board the aircraft.

As soon as we sat down in the airplane and fastened our seatbelts, a voice came through my senses, but it was not the hostess. No, sir. The voice said, "Now we have to visit your parents as soon as possible to tell them the good news and to get their blessings too."

The euphoria I'd experienced just a little while ago turned instantly to agony. I was in real physical pain. My stomach filled with unbearable knots, and my bowels churned with unbelievable speed. I broke into a cold sweat as BWIA flight 868 taxied the runway and the airplane made its upward climb. I grabbed onto the hand rests for dear life. Julie tried to broach the subject again, but I put her off, saying only, "Not now, dear. Leave it for later."

How much longer could I evade her? It was the most feasible request. After all, we'd both had the time of our lives with her parents. It was only proper and logical for us to duplicate the experience with my parents. Julie had inquired about my parents and siblings many times. Every time, I told her they were still living in England, and all was well.

All this time, I'd had absolutely no connection with any of my family members. I didn't know if they were alive. I didn't know if they were dead. Can you imagine that? My parents and siblings left me with my fake uncle and aunt and never turned back. I must confess I still had no idea if my dad was sending them money to take care of me. I doubted he was. I believed they had left me to live as a foster child.

In reality, all signs pointed to Ann and Eric as my adoptive parents.

CHAPTER 9

I was eleven years old when my family left for England. Eleven years old and sent to live with relative strangers. My parents and siblings missed all my growing up. They missed every major accomplishment in my life—and there were many accomplishments. My aunt and uncle were always there for me, but they couldn't replace my family. Deep down, something was always missing. As I write, I'm still having trouble trying to articulate the void I felt at that time. I used to be haunted by a never-ending nightmare. Out of four children, Sinclair was their albatross. I had to have done my parents some injurious harm they couldn't erase from their collective minds. In many households, the father might make a bad decision, but the mother would step in as a counterbalance. But in my case? No one said a good word on my behalf. I was furious. I was seething in my mind.

And if I flipped the story around? I was smart, so they decided it would be better not to interfere with my academic progress at the time. Fine. But they were living in England, the proverbial seat of learning. Wouldn't it have made more sense to, at least, bring me up to England to complete my advanced studies? I never understood the thought processes behind their decisions.

I thought of yet another scenario. When my family left, I was eleven years old, my older brother, Alfred, was fourteen, and my two sisters, Elva

& Marjorie, were eight and five. Not even my brother tried to stay in touch with me. He didn't send a letter, not even a postcard at Christmastime. Everyone I knew who had relatives in England received a box at Christmas with all kinds of goodies and toys—toys that were the envy of the neighborhood kids who did not have anyone living in England.

What was my excuse? Thus, I began to pretend that my auntie and uncle were my real parents. My biological parents gave me no choice. So, when I turned sixteen, I began calling my new parents Daddy and Mommy. It was not a far stretch because my fellow classmates had every reason to assume they were my parents. These were the only people they could associate with me. If I knew as much then as I know now, I would have asked to take on my uncle's last name, but I didn't. I had every reason to hate my parents. At the same time, I kept thinking there had to be some good reason for the treatment meted out to me. I was a confused soul. I tried to drum out the noise by excelling in sports and being an academic overachiever. I busied myself with as many girlfriends as I could possibly have. Most of the guys I grew up with turned to drugs or alcohol to cover up their shortcomings. I turned to romantic encounters.

Then I met Julie, the Bajan-Guyanese princess I was about to marry. Her request for us to visit my parents was bothering me. I had to find a way to tell her the full story. Keeping her in the dark was causing me mental torture and physical pain. According to one of the "old people" sayings, "It felt just as uneasy as a police boot on me corn." I had to find a way to spill my guts—for my own sanity.

I told my fiancé the entire story of my life, from start to finish. Or should I say from start to the point of our conversation? She listened with undivided attention. She was so riveted by my story that she never interrupted me. Not once. I kept my head bowed for the greater part of the story. One, to really concentrate on what I was saying so as not to miss any minor details. Two, I was totally ashamed to relay such a sorry tale.

When I was close to the end of my story, I slowly lifted my head. My heart was racing, and my pulse was exploding. I was trembling. My entire body was soaking wet like I'd just completed a spirit-filled, fully immersed water baptism. And tears flowed down my face. I threw myself into her comforting arms, and we cried. We cried. We just cried our eyes and our hearts out together.

I hope you believe me when I tell you after that experience, I felt so whole. After the embrace, we wiped each other's tears away with our palms and with our fingers. We stared into each other's eyes, and we erupted in gut-wrenching laughter, which lasted for almost a whole minute. It was a laughter that meant, "You made it, despite everything that happened in all of your yesterdays, and we are here together."

After that moment, we thought it the right and proper time to begin making plans for our wedding.

CHAPTER 10

Julie and I thought, at first, that we should have a small, intimate wedding. This proved to be an impossible task, though, because it would entail eliminating most of the people we'd gotten to know over the years. For example, my cricketing friends, my university friends from when I lived in Jamaica, and now friends from the Barbados campus.

Julie, as I said before, was well-loved, and her list of friends was twice as long as mine. Therefore, we were inclined to use a sensible process of elimination which still left a sizable and unmanageable number of virtual guests. We couldn't see a plausible reason to leave out any of our many friends from this once-in-a-lifetime celebration. We had no choice but to open the doors to a huge number of our friends. We needed them to come, to bear witness to our love, and to be part of our wedding day.

Handling the logistics of such a huge wedding proved to be extremely complicated. Our friends were coming in from all the different Caribbean Islands. There were vacation times to coordinate and flight schedules to manipulate. There were also hotel rooms and other means of accommodation to facilitate.

Julie and I realized early on that it would be a herculean task to oversee such a gigantic undertaking. Sane minds prevailed, and we decided to pass this burden on to a seasoned professional. We employed a wedding planner.

She and her staff worked around the clock, and after two years, the wedding announcement was made.

The day of our wedding dawned with one of those Caribbean mornings that God took his own sweet time to make. "One of those mornings" is exactly the theme local government officials used in commercials to lure millions of tourists into the Caribbean. There was not a cloud in the sky. The birds tweeted from one tree to another to serenade and announce a new day:

> *Morning has broken.*
> *The birds and the cocks have spoken.*
> *Leaves are dancing, the dogs are barking,*
> *Women are making smoke rise in the kitchen.*

It was not a holiday on the island, but everything and everyone moved at an abnormally slow pace. Even usually unruly and rowdy school children and busy, bustling shoppers seemed to be moving in slow motion. After all, it was our wedding day, and the heavens had shown their approval. We stood barefoot on the beach, and we committed ourselves to each other in front of God, family, and friends. At that precise moment, a friendly wave slowly and deliberately kissed us from the soles of our feet up to our ankles then it ebbed away. The water was warm. The feeling that oozed through my body was reassuring and comforting. I desired nothing more than to hear the preacher pronounce us husband and wife and hear his urging, "You may now kiss your bride."

This was a moment in time I will remember for as long as I live. Following the nuptials, a real West Indian jam session began. The music ran the West Indian musical gamut: reggae, zouk, salsa, and even European waltz. But when all was said and done, it was calypso music that played most frequently, and whenever it played, the patrons jammed the dance floor.

I remember dancing to calypso hits like "Dat Beach is Mine," "Fire Fire," "Black Man Come to Party," "Sugar Bum Bum," and "Jean and Dinah."

Are you wondering about food? All the West Indian delicacies were on glorious display. Pilau rice and peas, cook-up rice, lo mein, hard foul, chicken, pork, beef, crawfish, lamb, lobster, roti, buss up shut, saltfish cakes, crab, callaloo, and wild meat.

Drinks! You talk about drinks? Rum, rum punch, black wine, whiskey, brandy, beers from all the islands, sorrel, mauby, ginger beer, lime squash, and grapefruit and orange juice. Did I leave anything out? I don't think so.

Yes, I left out Ponche-de-Creme, Irish Moss, cask wine, and Guinness Stout. The West Indian saying was well represented: "Drink if you drinking." This was a real West Indian lime-- a jam session of epic proportions. Most guests referred to it as "the party of the year."

The party went nonstop from one in the afternoon to six o'clock the next morning. When we finally rolled into bed, it was nine in the morning. And we knew full well we had to be up by five o'clock in the following morning to catch the 9 a.m. flight out of Pearl's Airport. We were physically exhausted, mentally drained, and romantically giddy. We were on an emotional high, so we just laid in bed, unable to summon sleep to our weary eyes. We opted instead for passionate lovemaking.

The next day, we limped our way to the airport to get our honeymoon underway, which we would spend in Aruba.

Months before, when we'd made plans for our honeymoon, I was highly in favor of the Scandinavian or other European countries. My thinking was that we both had been born in the Caribbean and that we were both living in the Caribbean region. No matter which island we visited, either for business or pleasure, they all offered the same things—sand, sea, and sun. We both worked in Barbados, and we had visited St. Lucia, Grenada, Trinidad, and Jamaica, so I was not interested in any of these islands as a honeymoon choice.

For me, a honeymoon destination had to be different, first of all. It also, by my sensibilities, had to be exotic and romantic with a high degree of grandeur and sophisticated splendor. I thought we were in agreement about that, and all that was left to do was to choose between Denmark, Norway, or Sweden. Coincidentally, if it were possible, we could visit all three. My fiancé kept bringing home brochures about "The Other West Indies," as she referred to them. She seemed more concerned than ever to remind me of the very diverse, multilingual islands. She scolded me, telling me there was not just the British West Indies. There were also, she said, "The Spanish West Indies, the French West Indies, and the Dutch West Indies."

I replied with exasperation, "I know as much about West Indian history and West Indian geography as you do, so don't you lecture me. Besides," I insisted, "they are still sand, sea, and sun. We've been there, done that. There is basically no difference." I was out of breath by then. "I just thought for our first trip as husband and wife, we should go somewhere different. That's all."

I was livid. I was screaming at the top of my voice. I heard myself as if I were having an out-of-body experience or attending a séance. I didn't like it. Suddenly, I stopped myself.

In the three years we had been dating, this was our first real quarrel. A quarrel over something very trivial.

I quickly apologized and decided to let her have her way. "Aruba it is."

A wise and prudent man once said, "Happy wife; happy life." We were all lovey-dovey again, as we encountered our first real "make-up" (if you know what I mean). In case you don't know what I mean, let's just say I would be willing to have another quarrel as long as I was guaranteed a make-up like that one.

Once we got settled in our hotel room, Julie proceeded to tell me, rather hesitatingly, the real reason she insisted on us traveling to Aruba.

"I have a half-sister who lives in Aruba," she blurted out. At the end of that statement, a deafening silence filled the room. It was a silence so complete you could have heard a pin drop on the thickly carpeted floor.

"What are you talking about?" I tried clumsily to break the silence. In all our many previous conversations, she never once mentioned she had a sister, half or whole. She had always reveled in the fact that she was an only child.

Now I was confused. What could have changed? When did it change? Why couldn't she tell me before? I was in no mood to spoil our honeymoon, so whatever she said went in one ear and out the other. She composed herself and went on to tell me the backstory, whether I was interested in it or not. Well, to be truthful, she had my attention from the first words out of her mouth.

"My dad," she said calmly, "he lived and worked in Aruba when he was a young man."

"Aruba?" I said, "How did he get to Aruba?"

Then she continued, "My dad left Barbados with a group of guys right after World War II to work in the Lago Oil and Standard Oil refineries."

Julie explained that Lago Oil and Transport Company, Ltd. had its beginning in 1924 as a shipping company carrying crude oil from Lake Maracaibo to its transshipment facility on the island of Aruba. It later built huge refineries to refine its own oil. This called for a large base of mainly unskilled laborers. Many of these workers were recruited from other Caribbean Islands. That was how Julie's dad got to Aruba.

"He was lucky to be able to work his way up from an unskilled position to becoming part of the managerial team. After about ten years, there was no longer a need for those workers, so he took his savings and came home."

She could not miss this opportunity to take her bragging rights, so she teased me, saying, "That house we have in Barbados was built with Lago money. Later, he was able to capitalize on the managerial skills he'd been so lucky to acquire while working at Lago. This enabled him to get the job he now has in Guyana."

She went on to explain that while living in Aruba, he had "sown some wild oats" and had no idea he had fathered a baby during that period in his life of merry abandonment. "My dad went back to Barbados, met my mom, fell in love, got married, and had me.

"According to my mom, a few years after my birth, she received a letter from a young lady who was overly anxious to meet her estranged dad. From all indications, she was trying desperately to find her father. My dad said he knew nothing about fathering a child during his stay in Aruba, but he remembered having a sexual relationship with a woman. My dad further stated he was willing to take financial responsibility, and he accepted her as his daughter."

Her name was Dorothy, and she had planned to visit but was unable to make the trip. Julie reasoned, "We have exchanged letters and pictures, so I already have an idea what she looks like. I'm a little nervous, but I'm also preparing you to meet your sister-in-law as I'm preparing to meet my sister."

I listened without saying a word, though a million and one questions were churning around in my head. I asked myself, *why do West Indians have to move around so much? It is always the man. How does that affect the women in their lives? Could he have fathered more than one child? Who knows?*

Largo refinery

For these reasons and more, there always seemed to be something lurking in the dark. There was a grave and ever-present possibility that your lover could be your sister, but your sister had no idea or vice versa. Can you imagine?

While we were still in Aruba, we received an invitation from my best friend, James, to vacation in Trinidad.

But there was a caveat: we must visit to see and participate in Trinidad's Carnival. This two-day festival is known as the biggest street party on Earth.

I screamed when I read the invitation from James.

Julie ran into the room with a perplexed look on her face. "What's wrong?" She blurted out.

I stammered, jubilantly waving the invitation at her, "This is a dream come true!"

I told Julie about the numerous discussions and arguments James and I had every year about Trinidad's Carnival. We made many predictions, over the years, about which masquerade band would win Band of the Year. We wagered the sparse money we had on settling who would win the Calypso King contest.

After all these rancorous and contentious arguments we had many years ago, James and I would finally get a chance to see Trinidad's Carnival for what it really is.

No longer would we have to listen to descriptions of Carnival costumes or renditions of calypsos over the radio. We would be able to see some of our Carnival heroes, like renowned bandleader George Bailey, and calypsonian superstars the Mighty Sparrow and Lord Kitchener.

James was the obnoxious boy who challenged the authenticity of my intelligence during my first weeks in high school. We eventually became best friends and remained friends over the years through frequent correspondence.

James's family and my family had left us in Grenada and traveled to England to seek a better life. However, James was more fortunate than me as his parents eventually sent for him to join them while my parents never stayed in touch with me.

James completed his studies in England and graduated with a master's degree in civil engineering. He was employed by a very prestigious firm in London that had subsidiaries all over the world. My friend got to Trinidad because he was tapped to manage the company's subsidiary in Trinidad.

James was unable to attend our wedding due to conflicting circumstances with the demands of his job, so his invitation for us to visit Trinidad for Carnival was his wedding gift to us.

My wife and I decided to take him up on his offer, anxious to witness this eighth wonder of the world in all its gory details and spectacular splendor.

We landed at Piarco Airport on the Thursday afternoon before Carnival Monday, and we could feel the excitement as we sensed the urgency to let go of all our inhibitions. We drove through heavy traffic, throngs of people bustling and hustling at every turn. Car horns blared, flags waved, people collided on the narrow sidewalks. We were catapulted into the heart of the capital city, Port of Spain, and became immersed in its sea of madness. The smells of Trinidad's native dishes clogged the hot, steamy, stuffy atmosphere. We smelled curry, masala, and girah. The flavor of the dishes was on my tongue as steam billowed from the pots filled with rice and peas, baked breads, fried fish, and an amalgamation of other local delicacies.

Not long after, we succumbed to this flavorful onslaught. I ordered a chicken roti. My wife ordered the fried fish with gravy over a bed of rice and peas with steamed yams, green bananas, and sweet potatoes. My friend, James, ordered fried bake and shark.

Music was all around us too. The rhythmic, pulsating, bass-driven tempo of calypso music got into our souls. Our bodies moved to the beat impulsively and involuntarily. The combination of the aroma from the foods and the loud, booming music was enough to drive us out of our minds.

That's when James laid out the itinerary for the next six days—from Thursday right up until Ash Wednesday. He gave us strict instructions to sleep as much as we could during the day because the onslaught of activities would last all night, every night.

Here was James's itinerary:

FRIDAY: Soca Monarch Competition.

SATURDAY: Panorama.

SUNDAY: Dimanche Gras Show and King & Queens Costume Competition.

CARNIVAL MONDAY: Opens up with J'ouvert, which is the official start to Carnival.

CARNIVAL MONDAY and TUESDAY: Masquerade bands with thousands of people jumping in the streets in a blaze of colorful costumes

The revelry would end at midnight on Tuesday.

We thoroughly enjoyed the festival, replete with our costumes. We did it. We played mas, and we loved every minute of it. On Ash Wednesday, we went to Maracas Beach to soak away our aches and pains from a grueling seven-day fiesta extravaganza. Julie and I might never do this again, but it was the experience of a lifetime. We left the island of Trinidad feeling re-energized to take on our jobs with more vigor as we checked off our bucket list:

Marriage—check.

Honeymoon—check.

Trinidad's Carnival—check.

Trinidad Carnival Street Scene
(photo: shutterstock.com)

We had accomplished much in a very short time, but there were some more checks we were destined to make.

We left Trinidad determined to work harder and longer at our respective jobs. We concentrated all our energies on saving as much money as we could. We decided to forgo any more expensive vacations and cut out frivolous and unnecessary purchases. And we turned our attention feverishly to the most important item on our bucket list: starting a family.

Julie got pregnant about three years after we came back from Trinidad's Carnival. She was fortunate to be able to work up to the eighth month of her pregnancy without the dreaded morning sickness.

We started our family with Joey, our firstborn, who was a healthy, bouncing baby boy. Two years later, we expanded our family with the birth of our little baby girl, Sylvia.

We thanked God for the preparations we had made and that we were financially stable. This made it possible for Julie to be a hands-on stay-at-home mom. And our family was soon reaping the benefits of that decision.

Our jobs gave us access to the inner sanctum of the governments of Barbados, Guyana, and others, throughout the Caribbean. Although at that time, as I said before, I had given up on my parents, the same old question kept rearing its ugly head now more than ever before. I wished my parents and my siblings could "see me now." I was financially stable and wished I could do like some of my friends and buy them a home and take care of their needs. I was incredibly happy on the outside but extremely unhappy on the inside.

Most people don't know why they're unhappy, sad, or frustrated. However, in my case, I knew. The question for me wasn't why I was unhappy. Instead, my question was: How can I be relieved from this nagging unhappiness?

One day, I received a phone call from my Auntie Ann, which was a little unusual. Normally, Eric was the one to call me. Then he would let me talk to Auntie. Nevertheless, I was not too perturbed until she gave me the reason for her call. She was certain that Uncle Eric was becoming very forgetful. He'd lately adopted a nonchalant and unusually laissez-faire attitude. She was anxious to know my thoughts since she had never seen him in such a disposition. She went on to say that his doctor suggested a change of pace and possibly a change of place, a mini-vacation.

Before I could say anything, she jumped on the defensive. "Don't you go ahead and send us any tickets," she said. "We might as well spend the money we have here because God only knows—"

I interrupted, not wanting to hear what terrible things she might say. I ended the call abruptly, telling her to let me know when they would be coming. "We will be there to meet you. Bye, Mom. Give Dad my best regards."

As Uncle Eric and Auntie Ann walked down the tarmac, I couldn't help but notice that she was helping him more than usual. He looked very frail compared to the last time I saw him, but he was still in good spirits. He played with the grandkids and teased my wife about me and our highfalutin lifestyle. He also brought me a calypso album, and his face lit up when he said to me, "I just had to bring you that new album by the Birdie." He kept pointing to a particular track on the album. "As soon as you reach home, play track number four—you'll love it."

This was the Mighty Sparrow at his storytelling best. Uncle Eric and I sat and listened dreamily, our eyes staring at the spinning disc on the phonograph. We were hypnotized, both from the continuous spinning of the record and the realness of the story. The story was about "The Old Man, the Boy, and the Donkey."

This was a classic story from *Aesop's Fables* from the sixth century BC, reappearing in the *Harvard Classics*, 1909-1914. The Mighty Sparrow was able to put a modern twist on the ancient story. He used his intelligence, wit, and pizzazz, in combination with his awareness of his surroundings, to give new life to this old story. He gave the rendition of his adapted story his own interpretive moral, ending the calypso in an ingratiating way. The moral of the story is plain to see: "Please yourself because you can't please everybody."

After what we both construed as a great performance, we stood up and grabbed each other. Through hysterical laughter, Uncle spewed out, "Ah know you would like that one." He continued, lavishing praises on the Mighty Sparrow, ending with his favorite phrase: "Dat man is a master."

I replied, "A master, indeed!"

We spent two lovely weeks together. During that time, we took Uncle Eric and Aunt Ann to see the doctor. They both checked out fine, but the doctor suggested that Uncle should cut down on his workload. He also told them they should take little walks in the mornings, eat right, and rest more.

When it was time to say our goodbyes, Uncle Eric thrust a large brown envelope into my hands. "I have been saving this for a while," he whispered, "to give you at the appropriate time. I think the appropriate time is now."

He continued, looking me straight in the eyes, "Take good care of yourself and your family. Don't worry about me because no matter what these doctors say, when the man upstairs is ready for you, he's ready for you."

We said our goodbyes, then Julie and I embarked on the longest ride home from the airport. My wife and I glanced at each other every now and again, then stared down at the envelope. Not one word was spoken for the entire three-mile car ride from the airport.

The atmosphere was gray. The mood was black. We walked into the house like two zombies.

Julie decided to leave me alone to explore what was inside the envelope. I stared at it for a long time, afraid of its contents; I couldn't open it. Then I finally gathered enough courage to open the envelope and pour its contents out onto the floor in front of me.

A pile of letters lay before me. They were letters from my dad, written to Uncle Eric. I was shocked, amazed, dumbfounded, speechless—all these emotions rolled into one. Could this be the smoking gun? Could this be my vindication? Could this be the answer to all my prayers?

I read through the letters very quickly at first. Then I reread them slowly, repeatedly, until I was convinced that I was not hallucinating. I started screaming, "I knew there had to be a reason. I knew there must have been a good reason. I knew there had to be a reason . . ." I just kept repeating the phrase like a mantra: "There had to be a reason."

My dad reiterated on more than one occasion that he did not want to interfere with my academic or sporting achievements, so he wrote to my uncle, "Just let him continue to live with you. I owe you my life." In another letter, he wrote, "Please don't let him know the horrid conditions under which we are living. Please, please help him to live the life on the island that he'll never be able to live here. Not now, anyway."

Most people living on the islands thought that when people "go away," their lives automatically changed for the better. I'm sure this was true in many instances, but in my family's case, it turned out to be the exact opposite.

Amidst the overall bleakness, my father mentioned in one of his more recent letters that there was a little glimmer of hope. He mentioned that Alfred, my older brother, was making strides with his music, and he was now living on the continent. There was another letter in which he lauded my uncle for not leaving the island. "Look how well you've done," he wrote. "I wish I'd had the guts to stay. But it had become so fashionable at the time to travel to England that instead of trying harder with the little shop, I just picked up and left.

Now I realize what the old people used to say was true, 'The grass always looks greener on the other side.' England is no bed of roses, and if there are roses, there are more thorns between the roses."

He continued, "Let me be really honest with you, man, I want to come back, but I can't even begin to think about it. Firstly, I don't have the money to purchase the tickets for the airfare for myself and my wife back to Grenada. Secondly, if I do come back, everyone would be expecting to see me build a big house and drive around in a flashy car like a big shot.

"Well, I cannot do that. I don't want people who were in a lower class than me to have the opportunity to taunt me and laugh at me." The letter continued, "I could hear them gossiping, 'Is not so he was. Is so he come.'"

"Eric," he wrote, "I'd rather remain in England and die as a pauper than come back home for all these people to jeer and laugh at me. You may not believe it, but I still have my pride. You can call it false pride, but I am certain there is no way I'm coming back to suffer such humiliation."

CHAPTER 11

I was overcome with hurt and shame after reading all his letters. I made up my mind right then to take it upon myself to build my parents their dream home. They were going to come back home, and no one in the village would dare say or think anything demeaning or derogatory about them.

I was now back in touch with my parents after all these years. I got on my knees and promised God I would care for them and cherish them as long as I lived. This was the first time my wife and I weren't crying over sad news. We were jubilant. We were ecstatic. We behaved as if we had just won the Littlewoods Sweepstakes.

I called Uncle Eric, and the first words out of my mouth were, "I feel eternally blessed. I have two dads and two moms, and I will cherish the four of you as long as we all shall live."

"I am very relieved," he said after blowing out a deep breath. He echoed my thought, "God is good, all the time."

I answered, very reassured, "All the time, God is good."

That night, I wrote to my dad. I knew what I wanted to say, but my thoughts ran helter-skelter in my head. My pen refused to move as fast as my hand, and my hand found it difficult to follow the instructions from my brain. I paced the room for about half an hour. I sat down. I paced again. I sat down again. I went through these motions numerous times as if I were sitting on pins and needles. I eventually calmed down, sat down, and wrote to my dad—my real dad.

My thoughts poured out of my head, through my fingers, into my pen, onto the paper. By the time I finished writing the letter to my dad, I was drained. I had emptied myself onto twenty sheets of 8x10 writing paper. My letter captured all the years of wondering, all the years of frustration, all the years of simply not knowing.

All these years, mixed up inside me like a callaloo soup with anticipated excitement, gushed out of my brain like a billowing and angry river flowing relentlessly into the sea.

It was as if all the boulders were removed from where they had been perched for years. All the uprooted trees, all the sandbags, even some of the broken bridges were dislodged. Everything in its path had to be removed in a clean sweep. The only time the raging ceased was after depositing tons of wasted and unwanted garbage to its final destination. Then the calm would come. It was like going through internal cleansing. This purging harkened me back to my Sunday school days when the story of Jonah in the whale's belly had become my intense focus.

The Bible story states that after Jonah was thrown into the sea, a great fish swallowed him up. He remained in the belly of the fish for three days and three nights.

I had gone through my proverbial three days and three nights, and just as *"the fish vomited out Jonah upon the dry land,"* Jonah 2:10 (ESV), I felt as if I, too, had vomited out of my system all the hurt, all the anguish, and all the pain that had welled up inside of me.

I felt a great, indescribable relief. I felt as though a twenty-thousand-pound weight had been lifted off my body. I attempted to get off the chair and walk toward my bedroom, but I couldn't. My legs could no longer hold me steady. My knees buckled. My head became as light as a feather. My eyes watered, and my vision blurred.

I became paralyzed, unable to summon any physical or mental strength to move, not even one inch further. Suddenly, I slumped into my chair, and I slipped into the arms of Morpheus.

When I awoke, I felt like I had slept for days. I had no idea what day of the week it was. I was uncertain as to the time of day. Was it morning? Was it evening? Was it night all over again?

My wife later admitted she could find neither the courage nor the desire to wake me from what she described as "an unimaginable, peaceful, restful sleep."

Eventually, I realized it was truly morning. The morning was quiet—weirdly quiet. The birds did not sing, the dogs refused to bark, and the roosters took the day off. They didn't even try to awaken anyone. In this degree of unparalleled silence, I began to creep my way out of the groggy feeling that had slavishly engulfed me.

My body had gone through trauma. I felt sick. I was too weak to leave the house, so my doctor visited me at home. I finally began to heal, thanks to my wife's tender, loving care, and homemade remedies. I drank bush tea, spice tea, and ginger tea, and I was rubbed down with a concoction of grated nutmegs, a soft candle, and white rum. I now had every reason to feel on top of the world. So, with no more barriers in my path and a clear and happy constitution, I embarked on turning the dream of my parents' happiness into a reality.

For the next few months, I grew very busy, and I got lost in architectural plans, land deeds, excavation drawings, surveyor's reports, and bureaucratic red tape. We worked around the clock to get my parents' house built in as short a time as possible.

It took exactly six months from the turning over of the first spade full of soil to the last stroke of the painter's brush.

I was close to tears when I walked through the building for the final house inspection, but I smiled when the builder handed me the keys.

I clutched the keys close to my heart as I thought aloud, "I have built my parents their dream house, and I am extremely proud of this achievement. I have taken away the burden of shame from them."

I kept hoping this gesture would somehow restore their faith in humanity, albeit coming from their son.

CHAPTER 12

Every now and again, I sit and reminisce about the ritual accompanying West Indians' "going away."

It always involved a huge farewell party for the emigrant. The ceremony was a chance for the community to come together in one accord, to wish the traveler God's blessings, and to show the person how much they were cared for. In short, it was a farewell party.

On this occasion, the farewell party was for my dear friend, Eileen. I promised her that I would make a special effort to attend. I kept my promise.

Eileen and I had grown up in the same neighborhood. We attended the same primary school and had always been good friends.

She was born into a single-parent family. Her mother had to wash and iron for the more affluent families in the village to make ends meet.

I remember that Eileen was very popular in school. She was pleasant to everyone, and she always had a smile on her face.

Eileen got good grades, too, but making the transition to high school proved very difficult. Her mom was too poor to pay the tuition for Eileen to attend the only girls' high school on the island. At that time, I'd just received my scholarship when I was thirteen years old. Soon after, I left primary school and the village to attend high school in the city.

My departure left our friendship a little strained. But whenever I returned home on school vacation, we always made time to be together.

Eileen was seventeen years old when she left primary school. She was unable to find a meaningful job, so she doled out her services in helping people around the village.

Everyone, it seemed, knew and loved Eileen. She would sometimes cook and clean for families in return for a meal, hand-me-down clothing, or a small wage.

She would run errands for the elderly and the incapacitated. Apart from these regular and mundane chores, Eileen also took on childcare. She always seemed to be in her element when she cared for children. Many people thought she was the embodiment of a big sister. She was caring, attentive, and thoughtful. It did not take too long for this idea to take root among the villagers.

Everyone was soon calling her "Sister Eileen."

But in time, Eileen became intent on broadening her horizons. She was sure she could make something better of herself if only she got an opportunity to move away from the little village.

Eileen expressed her desire to travel to all her friends and even the people she worked for. It was no surprise the pervasive thought among most villagers was that their ills could only be cured by going away to England.

Eileen was able to borrow money from a few friends, promising to repay the loan with her first English job. A few people also started a petition in her name to raise money for her boat trip.

They raised enough funds in excess of the fare that they decided to throw a "Going Away" party for Sister Eileen.

This party turned out to be the biggest "Going Away" party the village had ever seen.

It began at about four in the afternoon, and people just showed up. Some came by invitation, and others strayed in. Men were busy in the backyard building the fire to accommodate the round-the-clock cooking required for a party of this magnitude. The men would find three big stones and set them in a triangular formation. They then placed pieces of wood in the middle of the stones and lit them on fire. Finally, a huge pot was mounted onto the three stones. There were three of these fireplaces set up in a section of the backyard. The triangular formation of the stones made it possible for the big pot to be perfectly balanced. This was done to ensure a continuous flow of food all night long.

Three or four women attended these stations. Their job was to make sure there was a plentiful supply of food throughout the ceremony. On the other side, adjacent to the cooking sites, three men would be stationed behind a mounted bar. Their job was to ensure a steady flow of drinks all night long—soft drinks for the women and children, and hard liquor for the men.

So, it was a real party. Everyone ate and drank heartily and merrily. Everyone would be talking, laughing, gossiping, and telling jokes. The attendees were in good spirits as they cheered up the person spending their last night with relatives, friends, and acquaintances.

This was the happy part of the ceremony; the sad part came next.

The local preacher had to be present for this second act. If he was late, someone was summarily dispatched to find him. The preacher would ask God for traveling mercies and to keep the traveler on the straight and narrow way. He urged them in his prayer never to forget those who sacrificed to find the fare, the clothes, and other necessities for their travels.

Escorted up front, the pastor laid hands on Sister Eileen, bringing down God's blessings. Then the crowd said a very audible, "Amen!"

Out of nowhere, someone started to sing the farewell song, the most appropriate song for such an occasion. It was the farewell anthem, sung at all farewell parties.

Its lyrics were terse, poignant with languishing overtones. Imagine a lone voice crying out in a sultry and deliberate tone, piercing the stillness of the night with its loving, haunting, and longing melody.

"Now is the hour
when we must say goodbye . . . ,"

As if they'd practiced and rehearsed a million times over, the voices chimed in obediently, warningly, admonishingly:

"Soon you'll be sailing
far across the sea . . . ,"

Right on cue, one voice began to wail as other voices hummed—a deep hum coming not from the throat but from the gut.

Grandmothers moaned. Parents bawled. Lovers sobbed. The words of the song were dragged out, and deliberately prolonged to exploit e-v-e-r-y syllable. Everyone hoped the traveler would hang his or her life onto every tear-stained note.

Then the lone voice returned to her designated role amidst the sad chaos. She sang pleadingly:

"When you're away,
oh, please remember me . . . ,"

SSome villagers gasped loudly. One woman said between her tears, "She'd better remember to send back me money."

Another woman said without apology, "Some ah dem does forget quick, quick, quick."

The first one couldn't come up with any more words, so she replied with a mournful groan, "Hmm. Hmm."

The lone singer continued, her eyes closed and her breasts heaving. Her right hand was lifted, way over her head, palm extended to touch the heart of Jesus. Her left hand was cupped over her left ear to give the words more resonance and true heartfelt meaning.

"When you return
you'll find me waiting there."

An old woman screeched: "By de time you come back, I'll be dead already!"

The women started to bawl. The men took stiffer drinks of rum—this time without any chaser.

Arms were flailing. Hugs and kisses and words of admonition were flying right, left, and center—all aimed at the traveler, Sister Eileen.

The atmosphere could be likened to that of a funeral. It was so sad, so touching, so moving.

The preacher, sitting with his eyes closed and his head bowed, was the complete embodiment of a man in deep, sincere, and peaceful meditation.

With no preamble or announcement, he caught everyone in attendance off guard when he shot up from his seat as if fired from a cannon. The preacher was on his feet, moving from side to side, when he let out a loud and agonizing groan and enjoined everyone to remain a little longer. He said the Holy Spirit had touched him and was leading him to deliver a special prayer for Sister Eileen.

The prayer came from deep within his diaphragm, and he eased up on his toes to get the push-start he needed. When he rocked back onto his heels, the prayer came out loud and clear.

"Lord, we know that many have left our shores, just like Sister Eileen tonight, looking to make it better. Not just for herself, Lord, but for those, she is also leaving behind. Touch her, Lord. Give her the strength to deal with that cold weather, Lord. Help her. Help her to walk in your light. Help her, dear God, as we pray and beseech you, Lord, in a special way. Go with her, Lord. Touch her with your blessings, Lord—from the crown of her head to the soles of her feet. Lord, let her feet be planted on solid rock, and to quote a line from a great songwriter, who was given the vision to write: Lord, plant her feet on higher ground. Amen."

In unison, all the people said a resounding and heartfelt, "Amen!"

They all joined hands around Sister Eileen, who stood in the middle of the circle. Their voices rang out with one happy accord as they sang jubilantly. Their sincerity was evident when they began to put more meaning to the lyrics than even the writer intended. They also injected the pronoun "her" instead of "me" to make it very personal for Sister Eileen.

> "Lord, lift her up, and let her stand by faith on Heaven's
> table land.
> A higher plane that she has found. Lord, plant her feet on
> higher ground."

That song was supposed to be an electrifying song, but the occasion was too somber. The weight of the ceremony was too heavy to lift the degree of sadness.

Some young boys stood on the periphery laughing, unable to see any reason for the sadness. As far as they were concerned, this should be a very happy time. One of the boys remarked exuberantly, "Ah can't wait for my uncle to send for me. This would be the happiest day of my life." He continued in a more serious vein, extending both arms to hug his friends, "Doh worry, man. Ah go send for all of you." Then faking an authentic English accent, he predicted, "Money's flowing like gold on the streets of London."

This engendered hysterical laughter from the group, and they dispersed. As the boys left, the people left the party too. A car passed that drew everyone's attention.

The male driver was wearing a tweed jacket with a shirt and tie. All four of his windows were rolled up as he drove by. He looked straight ahead, and at no time did his head move to the left or to the right. People began laughing hysterically, as one woman said to nobody and to everybody, "That is real stupidness. Since when we have winter in Grenada? Stupes." The woman finished, sucking her teeth.

Another person was quick to talk directly to Eileen, "I hope when you come back from England on holidays you don't forget where you come from." She looked vexed but continued, speaking of the man in the car, "Look at that jackass. He still thinks he's living in England. Ninety-nine degrees outside, and he's still wearing big jacket and tie, with car close up tight, tight, tight. This England does really make some ah dem get stupid for true."

She turned the rest of her comments directly to Sister Eileen. "Girl, just study you head, and don't end up as stupid as that damn man."

When the party ended, Eileen went home to finish packing her suitcase. She thought she finished, but her mom and some neighbors tried to make the already stuffed suitcase hold even more.

Ms. Emelda, Eileen's mom's best friend, rushed into the room with a glass jar in each hand and a bundle wrapped up in old newspaper under her left arm. She gesticulated with her mouth more than with her occupied hands. She managed to say to Eileen, "One jar is guava jelly, and the other one is damsel stew." She pushed her hand forward to show the jar in each hand.

"But there is no room to put all these things," Eileen protested.

Ms. Emelda moved her out of the way then sat flat on her butt. She pulled the suitcase closer to her and adjusted her legs until she could place the suitcase between them. She then proceeded to find room for the jars.

When Ms. Emelda tried to close the case, the cover did not come over far enough so the zipper wouldn't catch.

She yelled toward the kitchen for help to close the suitcase. Two heavyset women appeared and sat all their weight on top of the suitcase.

After a few minutes, Ms. Emelda shouted, "You all set, girl. You can't get that kinda jelly in England." She had a quizzical look on her face as though she was searching her mind for something. She finally blurted out, "How these white people call these things? Preserves," she said, rather mockingly. Then she rambled on, "So you have to make sure to take it with you."

CHAPTER 13

That night, Eileen did not even attempt to sleep. At 5:00 in the morning, the bus was in front of Eileen's door. She relied on two of her brothers to lift the heavier suitcases while the bus driver wrestled the other heavy case and the taped cardboard boxes. These boxes were filled with some of the island's exotic fruits, such as sugar apples, sapodillas, papayas, cashew plums, and golden apples.

In a matter of minutes, the bus filled with relatives, friends, neighbors, and a few well-wishers. It looked as though the whole village had woken up early to say their goodbyes. They all wished Eileen good luck and God's blessings.

This was what village life meant. Those were the days when the cliché was invented because it was so true: "It takes a village to raise a child." At that time, a parent could leave a child at home while they ran a quick errand, trusting the neighbor to "throw an eye for me." Neighbors shared everything: joy, sorrow, good fortune, and good food.

No one was surprised to see the level of support heaped on Eileen as she embarked on the proverbial path to fame and fortune. Still, she had to adhere to the constant and sometimes nagging reminders: "Never forget where you came from," "Please! Don't throw your life away," and "Don't forget to write your mother."

In the wee hours of the morning, the bus moaned and groaned under the weight of the many passengers, the huge suitcases, and the tied-up boxes. The driver had to be extra skillful, slipping the gear lever from third, to second, to first.

The bus needed the help of all the gears at different times as it gingerly climbed the steep hills and winding roads. He used the gears as the bus coasted down the steep declines and ambled around the curvaceous corners overlooking treacherous precipices.

This was Eileen's first trip to the city. She shared that she took in all the sights as the bus hastened through sleepy villages. She was accustomed to villages bustling with children on their way to school, laborers dressed in water boots with cutlasses, male store clerks sporting shirts and ties, and women in their prescribed uniforms. Eileen was surprised these places looked like ghost towns, except for the occasional stray dog. It was so early that some people were just saying their morning prayers, using the rosary as their guide. Others were saluting the morning with a good long stretch. Some households were busy lighting wood fires, adjusting the three stones around the fire to create a perfect balance for the pots placed on them.

Others were busy stirring up fires in order to roast breadfruit, sweet potato, and saltfish. Still, others were tending the pot on the fire, watching like hawks lest the cocoa tea boil over into the fire.

The bus skidded around the corner, and the tires shrieked, drawing Eileen's wandering mind back to the present. She held onto the seat as tightly as she could. Her mind moved in and out of reality but zeroed in, this time, on what might be in store for her on this boat ride of a lifetime. Eileen had never been on a boat before, and had no means of measuring what that might be like. She shuddered at the thought.

The passengers became lively when the bus driver pointed out the ocean liner in the distance. The huge boat was sitting there. Motionless. Deceptively still.

Eileen's pulse no longer pumped silently. Her heart began to beat so loud and so fast that she instinctively placed the palms of both hands on her chest to cover the spot and stop those who were sitting next to her from hearing the sound. There was a reason for the uptick in her heart's present disposition. She was scared, but she didn't want the friends, relatives, and well-wishers who had accompanied her to know how afraid she was.

She bowed her head silently, reverently. She closed her eyes and said a little prayer.

> *Dear God, I am so scared driving on this bus with all its twists and turns.*
> *How will I ever make it on this huge boat, on the rough seas?*
> *Help me, Lord.*

She ended her prayer in the way she'd learned from her Holy Communion sacrament classes. "Holy Mary, Mother of God, pray for us sinners now and at the hour of our death. Amen." She quickly lifted her head. With her right hand, she made the sign of the cross. She touched her forehead ("In the name of the Father"), then the middle of her chest ("and of the Son"), then her left shoulder ("and of the Holy Ghost"), then, finally, her right shoulder. Then she clasped both hands in front of her ("Amen").

The cross-signing ritual took about five seconds. When her eyes opened, she was no longer scared. A sense of peace and calm engulfed her.

There was now a sea of buses competing with each other and throngs of people on the docks. Buses came from every parish on the island. Each bus, like Eileen's, was filled with many well-wishers and a few travelers. As a result, there was massive confusion and pandemonium on the docks. At first, the drivers off-loaded the many suitcases and boxes to any empty space on the sidewalk so that the buses could drive to their designated parking areas and not tie up the traffic unnecessarily. No authority figure was present to give the buses proper instructions for off-loading the contents. After about fifteen minutes, there was a mountain of large wooden crates, leather cases, taped-up boxes, baskets, straw bags, large tin cans, and huge grips.

Where did these people think they were going? Did anyone tell them what they could or couldn't travel with?

Your guess is as good as mine. To be honest with you, it looked as though they were going to sell West Indian goods in a large produce market somewhere in London. Then again, it looked like some travelers had planned to have a sumptuous picnic onboard the ocean liner. Regardless of the hidden reasons or assumptions, one thing was certain. The message was loud and clear: these folks were going away, never to return.

It seemed to the very casual observer that they were taking all their worldly possessions with them, making sure to leave nothing behind. This was the overbearing element that made the scene so melancholy.

Parting was sad. Goodbye seemed to be forever.

For lovers, a kiss felt so extraordinarily weak. Not strong enough to withstand the impending separation, the pressure to keep intact what would now be a long-distance relationship. Many lovers were, for all intents and purposes, kissing their love goodbye.

A few feet lower down the Carenage, a wife cried and beseeched her husband to "Promise me you won't do me as what Michael did to Pam. Five years and is she and five children still catching she tail." She then looked up at him with pitying glances. "You promise to send for us as quick as you can. Please, please, don't let me turn old maid, and still waiting."

The husband assured her as best he could, but he had no way of knowing what the job conditions and the wages would be. He had no clue, but he did not let her in on his dark secret. He only reassured her he would keep his promise to her and the children, "As soon as ah can. Don't worry." In his heart, he knew this was a gamble. A complete roll of the dice.

West Indians traveling to London with baskets

(photo: shutterstock.com)

Every traveler took or gave their last hug. The people were lined up, every family with their designated traveler. The line seemed to take on a kind of order: mother, father, husband, wife, boyfriend, girlfriend, aunt, uncle, brothers, sisters, very close relatives, closest friends. Still, the activity made the scene feel chaotic, all these loved ones saying their goodbyes.

Alas, the docks were competing with the nearby sea. There was water everywhere and not a dry eye on the docks. It seemed everyone in attendance was bawling, crying, weeping, sobbing—openly and unabashedly. Water was everywhere. What a sight to behold; a most heart-wrenching sight.

After the travelers had hugged and kissed their relatives in the ascribed order, everyone gathered for the sendoff and waved their goodbyes in unison.

Soon after, the travelers were swallowed up in the bowels of the ship, as if boarding Noah's Ark. Some passengers on the boat wished they could change their minds and remain on the island. Some people on the shore wished they could change places with a passenger onboard.

But the time was nigh. The die was cast.

The sailors pulled up anchor, and the ocean liner silently plunged its bow into the deep, blue, expansive, and unpredictable ocean.

One by one, the buses left for their return journey, carrying one less passenger and much less weight.

CHAPTER 14

Suddenly, a woman sitting in the back of the bus groaned loudly and said for all to hear, "This is like a funeral."

One of the relatives seated upfront turned her head to address the woman. "How could you say that? We didn't bury nobody. She's just going away, that's all."

The woman at the back of the bus held tight to her point and replied, "That's exactly what I mean." She was in no rush to explain herself. Her speech was slow, firm, and methodical. She continued, "When someone dies, everyone goes to the cemetery with the deceased, then we all leave the cemetery and go back home. But we always leave someone in the grave in the cemetery."

The old woman blew out a deep sigh and shook her head a few times. The words came out of her mouth almost automatically, "Remember! Eileen came down on this same bus with all of us. But look, we are all going back home without her. Where is Eileen now? Eh?"

That last expression, "Eh?" was used to push her point deeper into the psyche of her listeners. She sensed that every passenger on the bus was convinced by her reasoning. She summed up her little talk quietly and confidently. "Like I say, it's just like a funeral."

The bus was silent. No one dared utter another word. Some fell asleep from the weariness of their sorrow. Some pondered the logic and the wisdom of the old woman's words. Some daydreamed as they tried to discern fantasy from reality. Some contemplated Eileen's fate. No one could know what would become of her.

The bus driver threw the gear lever from third to second to reduce the bus's speed. Then he eased the clutch down one more time and placed the lever in first gear as he prepared the bus to make its final stop.

This "going away" phenomenon is like a machete sharpened on both sides. Damned if you do, damned if you don't.

Like my dad wrote in one of his many letters to my uncle, "going away" represented a golden opportunity. You were not supposed to squander it, no matter the cost. "Going away" was a very traumatic experience for the entire community. For one, there was an expectation to send money back to clothe and educate your family and keep food on the table. Still, after a few years, you were expected to send for your children to join you: to expand and renovate the little old board house and upgrade the structure from wood to concrete.

Can you feel the intensity and the pressure the designated traveler went through?

Now you may understand why the West Indian is fully prepared to go to the ends of the Earth, if need be, to muster up a little respect and dignity for his family back home.

However, it must be pointed out that not everyone who traveled abroad looking for greener pastures found them.

Firstly, jobs were always difficult to find. The immigrant had to learn a new language, the new customs, travel routes, and other nuances about the new country. Because of this new status, even if he got a job, it was always at the bottom rung of the ladder. This meant his wages would be extremely low. Some other migrants had the good fortune to live, for the first three or four months, with a relative or friend who immigrated before they did. This meant that less money would be coming out of his check. He would have a head start on savings. On the other hand, the immigrant who was not that lucky had to take all expenses from that small paycheck and still find some money to send back home.

Most immigrants never moved beyond that last rung; after a while, they found it difficult to survive. Keep in mind that all these immigrants came from tropical climates. Dealing with cold climates took their breaths away. These immigrants became very frustrated and quite annoyed with their new surroundings.

The first solution that came to mind would be to return to their homeland. But how could these individuals really entertain such a thought? Why had they immigrated in the first place?

The dream of a better life had turned into a hideous nightmare. In some instances, the immigrant was lucky if he could depend on the state to place him on its unemployment list to receive benefits.

He might be given shelter plus a monthly stipend from the state government. He was at this point regarded as the scum of society. The immigrant might even be deported if he were assessed to be a financial burden to the state.

In either of the scenarios, the immigrant was totally disappointed in himself. In fact, he became a disappointment to his entire village.

If the immigrant was living on the "dole," he extricated himself from the local West Indian community. He would not want anyone to know it was impossible to find a job. If forced to go back home, he would be seen as less than a person; he would be judged as a total embarrassment. In almost all instances, he would be jeered at and looked down upon, and his life would be a living hell.

Instead of returning home to all this unpleasantness, the immigrant would content himself to remain in the alien country. He would prefer to deal with the cold climate, the uneasiness, the loneliness, and the homelessness. He involuntarily had to reject his family. Family members saw it as their duty and obligation to distance themselves from him and proclaim him persona non grata.

Now understanding the position my father found himself in, I garnered all my energy into finding out about my siblings. I had an older brother, Alfred, and two younger sisters, Marjorie and Elva, still missing from my life.

Finally, my parents were open with me about the whereabouts of my siblings. They decided to tell me as much as they knew about their different circumstances. In some instances, they even helped me contact friends and acquaintances of my brother and sisters so I could try to patch the pieces together.

From all accounts, my youngest sister, Marjorie, the baby of the family, had it the hardest. She had been six years old when they arrived in London. Because of her age, she blended into her new society very easily—too easily, some would say. She was the first in the family to master the new lingo, the very standardized and formalized way of speaking the Queen's English.

In fact, she began to think she was English, talking and giggling with her new friends. Then when she started grade school, she was immediately terrorized by the sheer majority of white kids. The schoolyard was a sea of billowing white faces—unfriendly and unaccommodating white faces.

She couldn't understand the constant verbal bullying. Marjorie became unnerved by the incessant name-calling with its accompanying "monkey and banana" references.

As she grew older and moved up in school, it became progressively worse. It soon accelerated from verbal bullying and physical harassment to pure mental torture.

It traumatized Marjorie. She began cutting classes and started hanging out with undesirable friends. Marjorie foresaw the dilemma her actions would bring. Her parents believed she was attending classes, but her report card would show her numerous absences. What could she do? She later confessed, "I had to do something, before something happened to me."

It drove her into the only survival plan that made her feel comfortable. She joined one of the notorious black youth gangs beginning to sprout up all over England. This was the only way she and several of her West Indian peers tried to combat the white racist anger spewing like molten lava from a once dormant white volcano. To quote a popular idiom: "It's dog eat dog, survival of the fittest."

At age fifteen, my youngest sister, Marjorie had enough. She left school. She left home. She pledged to live with, and for, the gang. She drifted further and further away into a very dark hole. She became steeped in a life of continuous and never-ending parties, hard drugs, and prostitution. And she soon reaped the repercussions of her deviant lifestyle. Before long, she was in and out of jail, fast becoming a hardened and seasoned criminal.

Then, out of nowhere, she was awakened and enlightened. Almost instantaneously, she removed herself from this punishing lifestyle cold turkey. Her amazing turnaround was so dramatic, so totally unexpected, that it was sometimes mentioned in the same vein as the unequalled conversion of the Apostle Paul on the road to Damascus.

It's amazing that after she reached rock bottom, one of her fellow gang members who had grown tired of the downward spiraling lifestyle to nowhere convinced Marjorie to turn her life around. They fell in love and finally decided to get their lives together. Marjorie abandoned the gang and started visiting our parents at regular intervals. She and her boyfriend were lucky to find jobs. This gave them a great chance to stay on the straight and narrow path.

At the urging of her boyfriend, they finally agreed to make a clean break from their past. They eventually decided to move back to the land of his birth, St. Lucia.

It was sardonically ironic that although he was born on the island of St. Lucia, he had no recollections of the place whatsoever. The simple reason was that his mother took him to England when he was two years old. However, he knew that he had aunts and uncles and other close relatives still living there. He never reached out to his relatives during all those years he lived in England. Nevertheless, because it was his mother's homeland, he thought that gave him some reason of entitlement.

He and my sister married and settled in St. Lucia with their only child.

On the other hand, my other sister, Elva, had a very normal life. According to reports I received, she refused to allow the lurking impediments all around her to hold her back. The rampant, glaring racism and verbal abuse only served as an impetus to make her study harder and become smarter than her tormentors.

She had her share of fights but was always able to physically take care of herself. She summed up the reality of those times in this manner: "I was never looking for a fight, but I wasn't running away from a fight either."

Elva was a fighter in every sense of the word. She literally fought her way through school. She persevered and received her first degree in accounting. Refusing to rest on her laurels, she was more determined than ever to prove a point. She put on her blinders and rejected the temptations buzzing around her to become more focused than ever on the task at hand.

She took the final exam and received a postgraduate degree in economics, having achieved what was at that time in England a gigantic feat. During that period, many black children were discouraged from even entertaining the thought of higher learning, so my sister's accomplishment was truly remarkable. She became a local celebrity. Black parents in England finally had someone to point their children to, and the black children ultimately began to see the dawning of a brand-new day.

Elva worked in London for a while. Then a few years later, she moved to Canada and became a professor at the prestigious McGill University. Elva also made appearances on the local television as an expert on financial matters. She remained single and had no children.

What about my older brother, Alfred? Was I ever able to locate him or find out about his life?

I remembered that my brother dabbled with playing the piano as a child. So, I was delighted to learn that he kept up his love for the instrument and became a piano virtuoso.

According to the reports I received, he played with many music groups until he formed his own band. When the band finally realized they were making slow headway in England, my brother moved with his band to the continent.

He spent years on the continent, never once returning to England during his sojourn. After he accumulated what he referred to as "enough money to live a comfortable life," he returned to England. He was more determined than ever to prove to himself and the world that he was a diverse and accomplished musician. He soon proved his mettle, and the critics were finally satisfied with his pedigree. His name became synonymous with excellence, and not long after, people started to search for the linkage between our last names. They remembered my prowess on the cricket fields in England, and it brought my brother and me full circle.

Wishing to cut down on the hectic pace of the music scene, my brother planned to settle down to a life of English gentility and respectability.

He never thought about going back to the island of his birth or any other Caribbean island. England was now his home. He reasoned that since he had lived in England for a greater period of his life than on the little island, he was now a bona fide Englishman. This assumption turned out to be premature after being introduced to an attractive and sophisticated Englishwoman.

Alfred was struck at first sight by her beauty. Her name was Effie. She stood 5'9"—a little shorter than his 6'2" frame. She was elegant and had a sharp sense of humor. Always fashionably dressed, she made her presence known whenever she walked into a room.

Their conversations readily revealed that her father was a black man born in Jamaica. He was the child of a white Scottish mother and a Black father, which meant he was classified by the locals as "Jamaican White." On further investigation, my brother also learned that her father came from a well-to-do Jamaican family. His grandfather was a government minister in Bustamante's political party, and he had carved out a beautiful life for his wife and his only son.

Her father went to England and studied to become a Lawyer. His prominence as a highly successful Jamaican in English society opened the door for him to meet and eventually marry one of England's high society ladies. Effie was the daughter of that marriage.

At first, my brother got no hint of Jamaican in the woman's stature or demeanor. But when she opened her mouth to speak, it became evident she identified more with her Jamaican and Caribbean roots than with her English and British heritage. She also had the knack of switching from the Jamaican patois into perfect English whenever the moment or occasion demanded it.

My brother said he was always amazed at how fluently Effie spoke the Jamaican patois. He was baffled by the ease with which this "White girl" danced to calypso and reggae rhythms. He was constantly surprised also at how knowledgeable she was about Caribbean politics in general and Jamaican affairs in particular. In addition to all these attributes, she was insanely intent on going back to Jamaica to do philanthropic work.

She finally got him to think along similar lines. He eventually realized, after much soul-searching, that he could by teaching music to some of the underprivileged kids in Jamaica.

Alfred and his fiancé started planning their wedding. The ceremony was to be held in Jamaica, on her grandfather's sprawling estate. All the relatives were contacted and given a one-year leeway period to make the necessary arrangements to attend. No excuses.

Two weeks before the nuptials, the island's daily newspaper ran this bold headline: "Jamaican–English socialite set to wed, musician, Alfred Ross, brother of former great West Indian batsman, Sinclair Ross."

My parents, sisters, and I all planned to touch down at Norman Manley International Airport.

Elated and overjoyed, I was curious and nervous to meet the family I once thought had abandoned me. I couldn't wait.

My parents flew in from Grenada and my wife's parents flew in from Guyana after a brief stopover in Trinidad for a few days. My younger sister flew in from Toronto, Canada. On her way over, she stopped off in New York to do some shopping. And my youngest sister, who had vanished off the face of the Earth, flew in from St. Lucia via Antigua with her Bohemian husband and son. My family and I flew in from Barbados.

One of our cousins, doing social work in Haiti, made a grand entrance, and a long-lost cousin flew in from St. Vincent. One of my mother's aunts now residing in Dominica, could not attend the wedding because her husband was taking over duty as the police chief. She was too busy with relocating, and her entertaining duties as the chief's wife got in the way.

Articles about this grand wedding plastered the pages of every leading newspaper on every island in the Caribbean. The blissful couple had planned to visit the French Caribbean Islands of Martinique and Guadeloupe for their honeymoon.

A few days before the wedding, I received a surprise phone call from my brother, Alfred. He thought we should spend some quality time together before the wedding. I jumped at this golden opportunity. He suggested we check out the wedding site, which was located a few miles from my hotel.

As I waited to be picked up, I began to feel a rush of buried and unwanted thoughts weaving through my mind. My brain was playing tricks on me.

Some of the hurt and anger I once felt toward my brother was trying to seep back in. I thought of bringing up the reasons for his disappearing act. I wanted to ask him a million and one questions.

One minute I wanted to know everything. The next minute I didn't want to know anything.

Only the night before, I had been elated, looking forward to seeing my brother. Now at the last minute, I wondered if I could change my mind. Could I come up with a plausible excuse?

These uncomfortable thoughts rushed over me. But as they ebbed, I became aware that I had already come to terms with it. Yes! I had forgiven my parents and my siblings. I was soon at ease with myself, and serenity pervaded my entire being. I was mentally, emotionally, and physically ready to meet my brother.

Before I could settle down with my new thoughts, who should appear but my brother, Alfred. When he saw me, we immediately recognized each other, even after an absence of many years. His overall body structure had changed, but when he smiled, the beloved dimples on his cheeks were still noticeable, although not as conspicuous as when he was younger. He threw his arms around me, and we tightly embraced for what felt like minutes.

Our embrace was reassuring, and I was sure we'd never let each other go. His head buried into my left shoulder, and my head buried into his. We said absolutely nothing. The tears poured out of our eyes like a stopper removed from a clogged-up kitchen sink filled with water. This was enough for us to realize how relieved we were to see each other again after all these years. We released our embrace. I cannot say who released first, but we stepped back and held each other's shoulders at arm's length.

His eyes traversed the length and breadth of my body a few times before he finally said, "Look at you! My little brother has grown almost beyond recognition." He smiled again. Then he said wistfully, "We have lots to talk about, little brother."

We ambled our way into the lobby of the hotel and sank into one of the soft, cushioned leather couches. I quickly gathered my composure because I wanted to be the first person to speak. Since I've wondered about and questioned my brother's lack of communication, I turned to him, deciding to be direct. I looked him straight in the eyes, and said, "You never wrote me, not even once! You never kept in touch; you never even tried." When I continued, my voice broke. "Because you never wrote, I could never write back."

He shrugged his shoulders and twitched uncomfortably in his seat. He could no longer look at me, so his gaze moved uneasily to an unfamiliar spot on the floor, then he hauntingly began to speak. "I am very sorry for not writing you or trying to contact you in any way. It's been a long time. A very long time."

He struggled to lift his eyes from the floor, still unable to look at me fully. His lips quivered, and his eyes blinked faster. He turned his body toward me instinctively as his voice rose just above a discernable whisper. "I apologize to you, from the bottom of my heart!"

After a few seconds, he took a deep breath, exhaling a sigh. The deep breath gave him some much-needed energy and a second wind, then he continued, "I was stunned when Mom and Dad decided way back then—out of the blue—to go to England. As you are well aware, they followed their usual modus operandi and made a wholesale decision for them and for us—their children."

Alfred started to get a little more comfortable. He adjusted himself in the chair as he turned his full gaze on me with a half-smile and intoned, "Initially, I was furious with them for making the decision to leave you in Grenada with Uncle Eric and Aunty Ann. I thought if they were able to find the money for the rest of us to travel, why couldn't you have traveled with us also? We all went to this land of opportunities, but the truth is, I was never comfortable in England. Everything was so different. The houses, the food, the people—these racist white people. Besides, it was always cold, and the skies were always gloomy and overcast. I began longing for the laidback, carefree life back home. Oh, how we took that life for granted. You could depend on the sun showing herself every day, intermingled with showers of rain. Never needing to wear a sweater, never having to queue up for the bus, never having people calling you disgusting and racist names to your face."

He took a deep breath again, but this time, he looked away from my gaze when he resumed with his explanation. "I began to take my rage and my frustrations out on you, although you were very far away from me. I kept asking myself, why does Sinclair have it so good? Why is Sinclair the golden boy? He is the smartest in the family. Is that the reason why he was the only one out of all his siblings to stay back in Grenada? I thought you were enjoying the good life while our sisters and I had to be pulled into that wretched place.

"My brother." He smiled wryly. "I have to admit to you, openly, that during my first five years in England, I hated you for these reasons and more. To add insult to injury, we heard all about your academic achievements while we were still struggling to find a foothold in our new environment. When you came up to England representing the West Indies cricket team, I lost it. My little brother was on the world stage. I am the oldest child, but I had nothing to offer, nothing to show. My life was at a standstill. I felt embarrassed to let anyone know that you were so great and I was a nobody. So, I told no one I knew you."

His eyes had this blank stare as if he was struggling to bring something into focus when the next few words tumbled out. "Remember what a nice house we had in Grenada? We had nothing in England but a crummy and cramped flat. To make matters worse, Dad got a job where he had to use tar and gravel to fill up potholes in the streets. Could you imagine our dad dressed in dirty, oily, grimy overalls, pushing a wheelbarrow across the streets of London? What a bitter contrast to the man our entire village looked up to. 'Good morning, Mr. Ross!' the people would greet him. They went out of their way to get close to him. On the other hand, our mom, the beloved seamstress, got a job in a factory manufacturing curry powder. As far as I was concerned, England stripped the dignity from our parents, and that made me feel awful and hateful. Dad, the respectable shopkeeper. Mom, the seamstress. I couldn't look at them the same way. I simply had to get away. I finally decided to follow my boyhood dream of becoming a musician, but there were always major obstacles in the way. Eventually, I summoned the courage and moved to the continent, away from my parents, my two sisters, and my friends.

"During that period of my life, I was a confused and unforgiving individual. I lashed out at everyone and everything for the simplest reasons. I was getting out of control. I developed an uncontrollable temper, and my health was unraveling beyond repair. I finally began to see a therapist at the insistence of a friend. The treatment was slow, but I steadily began to turn my health and life around. I got back to my music and became successful at it. The process took many years, but it paid off for me. That's my traumatic story. I'm sure Mom and Dad already told you about the girls and their ordeals."

Alfred was slowly getting back to himself. He had a full smile on his face, and he was sitting up on the couch, more comfortable than before. He leaned into me and said remorsefully, "Since then, I know you were never to be blamed for any of my pain, my chaos, or my confusion. I also want you to know I am very happy and proud of you, my little brother. I always was."

His face lit up with a big, wide, toothy grin. He pulled me up from the couch, and as we stood facing each other, he said exuberantly, "My dear brother, I hope we can let bygones be bygones and try to make amends for the many years we've lost."

I grabbed him in a tight hug as I anxiously told him I was eager for a fresh start. Then he pushed away unexpectedly and shook my shoulders, yelling excitedly, "Would you be the best man at my wedding!?"

I laughed and shouted back, "Yes! Yes! Thanks for asking me!" We ran out of the hotel's lobby, grinning from ear to ear like Cheshire cats, and sprang into the back seat of the waiting, chauffeur-driven Land Rover. We sat in the backseat, and it was as though we were in heaven. We talked and laughed with each other as we reminisced about the good old days. He remembered one particular incident when we were on the beach with a group of friends. The boys would dive underwater while the others would count to assess how long each boy remained immersed. The boy who was able to hold his breath the longest would be the winner. That day, the counting went on much too long for one of the boys. We all thought something was wrong, so we yelled for help. Instead of doing what everyone preceding him did, he surprised everyone by emerging out of the water a few yards from where we all gathered. He was shouting to us exuberantly, "I am over here! I am over here!" We were all very annoyed with him, but after a few minutes, we all joined him and were consumed with unstoppable laughter.

Alfred retold the story amidst fit-like spasms of hysterical laughter. He doubled up with pained laughter whenever he remembered the funny parts of the story before he was able to tell me. He slapped his leg, punctuated with high fives to me before he recalled the story in its entirety. Between fits of sporadic laughter and ensuing tears, he was finally able to piece together the long-forgotten and now newly remembered episode. The details of the story seeped back into my memory, too. I listened to his enthusiasm, and it evoked gut-wrenching laughter from both of us. The chauffeur checked on us through his rearview mirror but hastily decided to let us have an enjoyable time.

So blinded by our uncontrolled laughter, we were unaware the chauffeur steered off the main drag onto a dirt road that led us to the estate. The narrow strip was engulfed on both sides by overgrown vegetation. Our driver pointed out mango trees, mini orange groves, banana plantations, sugarcane, and other tropical trees. We spotted men and women in between the bushes. Some were planting, some were chopping down shrubs, and others were pruning. Our chauffeur was nice enough to stop for a few minutes to allow me and my brother to enjoy some coconut water from freshly-opened coconuts. It was exactly what we needed to cool down under the extreme Caribbean midday sun. That is when I noticed, for the first time, that the chauffeur was replete in a black suit, black bowtie, and black cap.

I instantly started to poke fun at my brother. "I know you're marrying up," I teased, "but this is way passed up. The sky seems to be the limit, big brother."

We high-fived each other and laughed louder than we did before. I continued to tease to no end.

Suddenly, the dirt road gave way to a paved road leading up a steep hill. Short, well-groomed palm trees lined this asphalt road, beyond which we saw meticulously manicured and well-watered lawns. The grounds were immaculate. I couldn't take my eyes away from the grandeur. I am tempted to ask you to close your eyes and imagine the opulent scenery, but you cannot close your eyes and read at the same time. So, take my advice: read first, then close your eyes and see through your mind's eye these fabulous grounds I'm describing.

We drove up the steep hill, the engine of the Land Rover crying its way to the top. When I looked up, I saw the roof of the mansion peeking out from between the dense green leaves. Its red galvanized top reflected the sun's midday brilliance. As the car inched up to the top of the hill, the entire building came into view. The mansion stood there in all its magnificent, splendid, and breathtaking beauty. Verandas extended across the front and sides of the house. Oversized windows boasted wooden jalousies, and the wooden lattice fences reminded me of an edifice to a bygone era of greed and gluttony exhibited by the slave masters—the original owners of this great house. The home was beautiful in every way, yet blighted by the scourge of slavery and the blood of my ancestors, a yesteryear that was sometimes difficult to forget.

I was lost in wonder and bewilderment when a young, black serving girl, garbed in a starched white apron and nurse's hat, broke the silence. "Lunch is served, sir."

I couldn't help thinking, between forkfuls of rice and curry goat, that in a few days, we would be stepping all over these once-sacred floors, unconsciously trampling out the old vestiges of slavery that still lingered. After lunch, the butler dutifully took us on an exhaustive tour of the mansion and its grounds. He assured my brother his wedding reception would be truly memorable.

We were driven back to our hotels, tired after a long day. That night, sleep did not come easy. I tossed. I turned. I saw disturbing images of my sisters, Marjorie and Elva. I began to think seriously about my sisters. I had confronted my brother, who was the eldest sibling, but what about my sisters? They were both younger than me, so it should be my responsibility to reach out to them. I reasoned I couldn't wait until my brother's wedding day (in less than three days) to see them for the first time in so many years. I had to see them before the wedding day. My dad told me the name of the hotel where they were both living.

The next morning, I called on them.

My older sister, Elva, recognized me and ran to me with outstretched arms. Marjorie, my youngest sister, was a little tentative with much less emotion.

"It's so good to see you in the flesh," Elva gushed. "I thought, on many occasions, that we would never see each other again." However, she was quick to philosophize, "I can finally put meaning to the old people saying, 'Two mountains would never meet, but there is always the possibility that two people will meet.'"

Elva couldn't stop smiling, but she abruptly realized how selfish she'd been through the entire meeting. She was so lost in awe, amazement, and disbelief that she was oblivious to Marjorie standing next to her, a few inches from me.

Marjorie vehemently butted in by claiming, "You can't take him all to yourself. I want some love, too." She grinned. "I've missed him as much as you have." She threw herself into my embrace, her arms hugging my neck, and whispered in my ear, "I really missed you. It's so good to see you again."

She released her tight grip. She looked at me from the crown of my head to the shoes on my feet, not missing any part in between. She simply said, "God bless my eyesight!"

A few seconds later, I was gleefully sandwiched between my two long-lost sisters. The guilt, the shame, and the feeling of not knowing leaked out of my entire body. I felt relaxed. Instantaneously, I was a new man. When I left my sisters' room, I was so light in body and spirit. I felt like I was walking on air. I skipped across the roadway to the parking lot. I jumped into the taxi and was so visibly happy, it compelled the driver to make the wrong assumption.

"She must have been extra special to you tonight," he quipped. "I can see she made you the happiest man alive."

"True!" I blurted out, bypassing his reasoning and unleashing the entire saga concerning my sisters and me. He was taken aback by my story, but he empathized with me. He ended up being such a good and sympathetic listener I gave him a hefty and well-deserved tip. That night, I slept like a baby.

The following morning, I was quiet and well-rested for the most part. I went to the barber, then I prepared for my brother's wedding the next day. Alfred's wedding was a spectacular and momentous event, the likes of which the island of Jamaica had not seen in years. The ceremony was solemn but very rich in religious tapestry and pageantry. I felt very privileged and highly honored to be upfront on the altar with my brother, Alfred. All the hairs on my head and all over my body were standing on end. I wasn't the one getting married, but I was more nervous than the groom. I had to pinch myself, literally, to be assured I wasn't experiencing a colossal nightmare. It was true. I was my brother's best man. I was the main witness to the beginning of a new chapter in his life.

The guest list boasted a Who's Who of Jamaica's illustrious society and neighboring West Indian Island societies. Let's just say that the guests represented the West Indies region's crème de la crème: politicians, educators, cricketers, musicians, doctors, teachers, nurses, reggae artists, and calypsonians.

The wedding reception was a blast. The beautiful, opulent grounds surrounding the magnificent and ornate mansion were in direct competition with the well-appointed decorations, immaculate place settings, mouth-watering West Indian cuisine, and appetizing desserts. The live band kept the guests on the dance floor all night long, asking for more. The word "extravagance" would be too mild a word to describe the entire jaw-dropping festivities befitting royalty.

My brother's wedding was a unifier: a glorious and momentous occasion for our entire family.

We were born into one family, but fate had taken us away from each other and scattered us all over the world. Then the same fate rejected the untoward circumstances and lovingly brought us all back together again. We were also united in our desire to spend time together. Everyone made sure the family had sufficient time—just the six of us—absolutely no intruders, not even husbands, wives, or the children.

We hugged, we laughed, and we cried. But most of all, we talked, we talked, and we talked. We also made sure we exchanged telephone numbers before we parted ways.

This was such an incredible situation. After all, so much time had elapsed since we had all stood in the same room together. Everyone was now grown, and we still knew deep down we had so much life to look forward to.

We got on our knees as my father thanked God for his enduring mercies on our family.

"Thank you, Lord, for seeing us through trying times. Thank you for bringing us back as the family you always intended us to be. Lord! We are indeed eternally grateful, and as the Psalmist says in Psalm 116, verses 1 and 2: *I love the Lord because he hears my prayers and answers them. Because he bends down and listens, I will pray as long as I breathe!*'"

When my dad's prayer ended, we all murmured a resounding, "Amen." We got up from our knees, feeling refreshed and rejuvenated. We were convinced that God had allowed us to survive life's greatest traumas, and we knew we would be dependent on Him to care for us in our future undertakings.

My youngest sister was the last to get up. She stood very gingerly, with both hands upraised, and said simply, "Our God is awesome."

We looked at each other and agreed. We said in unison, as if prompted by an unseen conductor, "He is awesome! Awesome!"

Do you know what the most rewarding outcome was? Would you believe that we never mentioned the past in any disparaging way? We were only overjoyed by the privilege to have our original family members present. What a blessing! That night as I watched my father, I saw again the moment he'd reunited with his homeland. I remembered his ecstatic words: "THIS IS PARADISE!" This image refused to leave my thoughts.

My father's experience working and trying to make a life for himself and his family was horrendous. Living in London, he was exposed to the hustle and bustle of the everyday English life. He saw the bright lights of a metropolitan city. He knew the grind of trying to make it in a foreign land. And it took a physical toll on him.

Looking at my father that night, I saw an image of the old man. The similarities didn't end with their physical qualities. My father was grateful he was able to return to his homeland. "Not in a box," he'd said, "but still able to relish and enjoy the unsurpassed beauty of my island paradise."

CHAPTER 15

When I was a boy, my family lived near the sea. Most mornings, I walked to the water to take a quick dip before going to school. As a member of the track team, I was encouraged to run in the surf, the swell of the sea that breaks upon the shore, to improve my leg strength and my speed. If I had a bruise or a scratch or cut, some extra healing power from the seawater would cure it in a short time.

Once, my friend's mom had a stroke. The doctor suggested she take a "sea bath" as part of the therapeutic treatment. We had no access to wheelchairs then, so I had to help my friend carry buckets of seawater to his house so his mother could have her sea bath. I almost forgot to mention that the bulk of our protein diet came to us from the sea. We ate fish every day cooked in every way: fried, stewed, steamed, or roasted.

The fishermen went out early every morning and returned home late at night with boatloads of assorted fish: barracuda, dolphin, flying fish, jacks, and others.

Some days when the catch was plentiful, the locals saved up for a rainy day by "corning" the fish. The vendors soaked the catch in salt, strung them through the mouth with corn straw, and put the fish out to dry in the sun. This was the way the locals preserved their fish.

We ate fish almost every day, while we hoped that one of the butchers would get lucky and kill a cow, a goat, or a pig. This was rare, so eating meat became a luxury associated only with the Sunday family meal. Villagers would say this happened only once in a while.

Living so near the water, we understood the nature of the sea. During the sunny season, the sea was calm. The water receded, and the tides were low, thereby exposing more sand and beach. As kids, we frolicked in her calm, balmy waters every day for hours on end. When the rainy season came, the sea became rough. We would no longer play carelessly in her choppy waters and billowing waves.

The fishermen couldn't go out as often, so everyone went into their storehouses for the corned jacks and the corned flying fish, which they'd preserved during the times of plenty.

We were taught as children to have total respect for the sea. We did. We had to because she demanded our respect. Then I either read somewhere or overheard adult conversations about tidal waves. I was petrified at the thought of them.

Grownups spoke of it as a meaningless phenomenon because, they concluded, "These kinda things happen overseas, not here." The little I had heard about them, though, was enough to keep me awake at night. I was frightened at the possibility of a tidal wave because of our close proximity to the water. I knew firsthand that our little island could easily be swallowed up by the sea. My entire family and I could be gobbled up.

One day, I stood on the shore with my back toward the sea. I looked up and saw the lush greenery, the hills, and the mountains. Then it hit me in the pit of my stomach: if ever there should be a tidal wave, I would wake up the entire family and run for the mountains.

I thought we would be safe so long as we could get to higher ground. I deduced that the higher we got, the harder it would be for the waves to climb over the mountains and wash us away.

This is how I think of the West Indians' never-ending quest, carried on from generation to generation. They keep searching to feel whole. Their search for opportunities to make their families great, always longing for dignity. They are continually running away from a tidal wave of entrenched poverty and destitution.

At first, West Indians left their homes and ran away to bigger islands. Then they ran away to places like Panama to build the railroads and the Panama Canal. They ran away to Aruba to work at Largo Standard Oil Company. They ran away to Venezuela, Cuba, and Santo Domingo to work the sugarcane fields. The West Indians kept on running to England, Canada, and the United States of America.

(photo: shutterstock.com)

We West Indians ran away to anywhere we could find the dollar, not just for ourselves, but also to send back home to our families. Our main obligation was to help those we'd left behind.

We want to find that reason for living. We want to know the joy that comes with finally earning enough to take care of the little necessities of life. There's no lust for "too much," only a simple longing for *enough*. West Indians want to taste the joy of feeling like a "somebody."

The perils of West Indian life can be summed up in two words: *running* and *searching*.

For some, the running is finally over; for others, the searching seems endless.

Thank God for those who finally find their higher ground.

CHAPTER 16

I have described how West Indian people have run from place to place to eke out a decent life for themselves and their families. The sad reality is that the running from place to place is inextricably tied to our disastrous history.

Black people were taken against their will and scattered across the West Indian Islands and the Americas. The explicit reason for capturing men and women from this one race of humanity was to provide the White man with a free, inexhaustible labor force.

The Black man quickly proved he was physically and mentally stronger than the White indentured servants who came before him.

The White workers died in unparalleled numbers, unable to withstand the heat, the bushy and mountainous terrain, and the deadly tropical diseases. But the lure of profits and sustainable wealth drove the White businessman into the depths of the largest continent to rape, pillage, and capture an entire civilization. They saw the Black man and woman as specimens able to resist the tropical diseases and the wear and tear of harsh physical punishment and gruesome pain.

I can only imagine the White man thought: *these people are like beasts. They must be able to work for long hours and to carry heavy loads for long distances.* Thus, their conclusion was: *we have to treat these savages as beasts.*

So, the White man proceeded to capture and treat the Black man and Black woman as they would a cow, ox, donkey, or any other dumb animal—an animal with no conscience, no feeling, no intelligence.

The White man's mind had to be in such a mentally deranged and depraved state that it became normal for him to herd Black people like animals. The Blacks huddled in overcrowded boats with chains and irons around their necks, wrists, and ankles. These precautionary methods were taken to transport this human cargo on the dangerous voyage across treacherous and stormy seas. In this way, they could be certain their captives would not jump overboard.

We, the Black race, were entirely different from the White race, but they still held onto their conclusions.

They were White and frail. We were Black and strong.

They were White and thought they were the first race. We were Black, so they thought we were the uncivilized race.

They were White and had money and power. We were Black and poor; we were powerless.

We worked their plantations. We were their slaves. In return, they became rich. We became poorer and poorer; they became richer and richer.

Because of his utter greed, the White man continued to plant the same crop in the same soil as long as it remained profitable. But, alas, the soil became depleted of its rich nutriments due to overuse. This resulted in a less nutritional product, a less marketable product, a far less competitive product.

The White planter saw his profits drop appreciably because the lands were no longer profitable. The Black people he had forced and coerced to work these lands for free for all those years were no longer beneficial to him. The lands were of no more use.

The White planter abandoned these huge estates and ran back to Europe with unbelievable profits. In this way, the era of Black slavery ended haphazardly. The slave was put out to pasture, just like an animal. What was the Black man to do? His mind, his body, and his soul had been conditioned to this slavery mentality as a way of life.

Could he just switch to another cycle? Could he just click over to new data?

The Black man faced a conundrum. To say that his mind was confused would be an understatement of the highest order. Black slaves were locked up in worse conditions than pigs corralled in a pen. They were caged with barbed wire fencing, their menacing and whip-happy masters always very near at hand. While all this loathing pervaded the closed slave society, there was a whole other world out there.

This "other" society consisted of legislators, entrepreneurs, traders, builders, etc. In other words, there was a society divided and subdivided by class, wealth, and color.

If the Black man were to venture into town, in which category would he be placed? The strata dictated he belonged at the bottom of the heap, the same exact position he was forced to assume as a slave on the plantation.

No matter where the Black man went, his status remained at the bottom. On the plantation, he was a slave. In society, he was merely a free slave.

The free society was scared and intimidated by this big, burly, angry Black man. Thus, society began implementing different means to continue to keep the Black man in his place—down. It was easy for the white man to perpetuate this domination. After all, the Black man was entering this new society with a million and one deficiencies. He could not read. He could not write. He had no critical thinking skills. He knew nothing about math. He had no language skills. He had no proper attire, no shoes on his feet, and no clothes on his back.

What a calamity. But regardless of his new status, he had to make a way where there was literally no way. He had to cut a road where there was only thick brush, huge trees, and immovable boulders. If he couldn't move these obstacles, he had to find his way around them. And yet, little by little, he did.

The four hundred or more years that the Black man was compelled to slave for the white man officially ended in 1838. Thereafter, the Black man had to turn to the only thing he knew for survival. He had to continue to work the land.

This time, workers devised a scheme with tiny, rented plots. One planted corn; Another planted yam. And they bartered with each other. After some time, another one started fishing and extended the bartering scheme.

This group of Black people remained, building small communities among themselves. Then slowly, ever so slowly, they began venturing into towns to look for work, to help themselves and their families.

RIGHT THERE. There began the migratory journeys of the West Indian people, which have continued up to this day.

By the 1900s, Black West Indians were becoming a little more accepted into the larger society. But what could they offer? What skills did they have?

They parlayed their strengths and hardworking credentials to obtain manual jobs. For example, the men found work off-loading cargo ships. Others worked with builders and construction companies, which required them to lift and carry heavy materials. The women began to show off their skills in cooking, baking, washing, ironing, and scrubbing floors.

Still, they used these skills working in the kitchens of the white members of the wealthy class. They worked hard, but their wages remained insufficient to maintain a family.

Some found their way out, but for those left working on the estates, life was incredibly difficult. The laborers, only a step up from being called slaves, were now paid by the white owners, but only a mere pittance.

The owners cleared their consciences by saying to all and sundry that there was no longer free labor. They guaranteed that every worker on the estate was a paid worker. On the other hand, the laborer argued that moving from zero to one cent was too close to zero to make any significant difference. They were paid what was tantamount to slave wages.

The Black West Indian man grew tired of this subzero existence. He argued that during slavery days, provisions were made for menial food, shelter, and clothing. Now, with a wage, he could not afford to provide adequate food, shelter, or clothing for himself and his family.

He had to devise some other way to tackle life. So, whenever he heard through the "Black telegram," the pay was a little higher on a neighboring or faraway plantation, he headed there. When he heard there were major projects on a neighboring island, where the wages were significantly better, he plotted to get there. He scrimped and saved to come up with the money to pay his way there.

In many instances, when it was too impossible to raise the money to pay his fare, he wandered around the docks for weeks, even months. He would then jump at the slightest opportunity to stow away on a boat to get to the desired destination.

This is how the constant migration began and has morphed into a never-ending journey.

There is no documented empirical evidence to support the notion that the West Indian loves to travel. He travels because he is compelled to do so.

The West Indian has always been forced to search for higher wages. To search for recognition and to search for dignity. The search could be for one of the above, or all of the above.

We are simply: "SEARCHING FOR HIGHER GROUND."

ABOUT THE AUTHOR

George A Glean, Sr., was born on the island of Grenada. He traveled to the United States of America, where he and his late wife, Denise, founded the Pre-k, kindergarten school, Children's Corner. Mr. Glean is a teacher and a consummate student of West Indian history. In addition, he co-produced, wrote, and narrated a radio documentary called "History of the Caribbean People," for which he won the prestigious award from the New York Association of Black Journalists. He has three children and seven grandchildren. Like many born in the Caribbean before and after him, George, the young man from Grenada, searched for higher ground and landed on Long Island, New York, USA, where he still resides.

www.ingramcontent.com/pod-product-compliance
Lightning Source LLC
Chambersburg PA
CBHW060332310726
48976CB00007B/2532